Sort of Forever

ALSO BY SALLY WARNER

Dog Years
Some Friend
Ellie and the Bunheads

Sort of Forever

Sally Warner

ALFRED A. KNOPF   NEW YORK

*for Claire, of course,
and for my friend Debbie Schwartz,
who was also there*

THIS IS A BORZOI BOOK PUBLISHED BY ALFRED A. KNOPF, INC.

Library of Congress Cataloging-in-Publication Data
Warner, Sally.
Sort of forever / by Sally Warner.
p.   cm.
Summary: Twelve-year-olds Cady and Nana explore the strengths of
their special friendship as they cope with Nana's cancer.
ISBN 0-679-88648-6 (trade). — ISBN 0-679-98648-0 (lib. bdg.)
[1. Cancer—Fiction. 2. Best friends—Fiction.
3. Friendship—Fiction.] I. Title.
PZ7.W24644Sr   1998
[Fic]—dc21   97-33367

Printed in the United States of America
10 9 8 7 6 5 4 3 2

KENNEDY

Contents

Prologue

"SHHH," NANA WEBER SAID, GIGGLING. "Did you bring the bottle opener?"

Cady Winton pulled it out of the pocket of her quilted jacket with a flourish. She waggled it between her fingers, and chrome glinted in the moonlight. "Ta-dum!" she announced in a loud voice.

Nana grabbed Cady's sleeve and tugged her toward the shadowy center of the vacant lot. She glanced nervously at the holiday-decorated houses around them. "Shhh," she said again. "You're going to ruin everything."

"Okay," Cady mouthed, quieter. She took a deep breath and looked down the hill at the lights of Los Angeles. They shimmered and winked, seeming extra bright in the cold December air.

"Well, are you going to help me, or not?" Nana said, sounding a little breathless.

"Oh. Sorry," Cady said, and she stuffed the opener back in her pocket. She grabbed two edges of the old scratchy navy-blue blanket Nana had brought, and the girls arranged it on the ground.

"This isn't going to be very comfy," Nana grumbled. "And the grass is wet."

"Don't worry, we aren't exactly moving in," Cady pointed out. "Come on, sit down. I'll open the sparkling cider."

"Let's call it champagne," Nana said. "From now on, I'm always going to drink champagne on my birthday. Maybe in between birthdays, too."

"Oh, great," Cady said, rolling her eyes as she struggled with the bottle opener. The cider cap flipped off onto the blanket, and a wisp of carbonation vapor rose into the air.

"Yippee!" Nana cheered in a tiny voice.

"Okay, where are the glasses?" Cady asked, looking around.

"I thought you brought them," Nana said.

"No, I thought *you* brought them," Cady said.

They stared at each other, and then, after a second, they both started laughing. "This is just perfect," Nana said between giggles. "Now we'll have to drink our fake champagne out of imaginary glasses. Happy birthday to me!"

"Shhh," Cady warned her. "I want to make a toast—*before* the neighbors come outside and chase us away."

"Okay, then, toast!" Nana said, shivering a little. Her eyes shone as she waited for Cady to speak.

Cady cleared her throat, sounding important, and raised the bottle of cider in the air. "To Nana, on her twelfth birthday," she said, as if to an invisible audience. "Too bad she was born two days before Christmas, or she could have had a party—with real glasses and everything."

"Don't forget that I'm having a party in January," Nana said, interrupting the toast. "You might even get invited," she added. "If we're still friends then, I mean."

"Ah yes, friends!" Cady said, lifting the bottle once more. "Thank you for reminding me. I have known Nana since we were darling little babies," she said to the empty hillside, continuing her toast. "Well, *I* was darling, but she was kind of smelly," she corrected herself.

"Was not," Nana said, laughing again. "That was you."

Cady made a show of ignoring her. "And all through the early years, our friendship lasted," she continued.

Nana snorted. "The *early* years?" she said. "What is this, the History Channel?"

Cady put on her most indignant expression. "Do you *mind?*" she asked, pretending to be offended.

"Sorry. Go ahead," Nana said.

"Okay, where was I? Oh yes, the early years," Cady said. "Yes, our friendship lasted all that time, and it will keep right on lasting." She took a swig of the cider.

"Yeah," Nana said, reaching for the bottle. "Our friendship will last—until we have some big old fight."

Cady thought about this. "But what would we fight about?" she finally asked. "I mean, we've made it this far."

"Oh, I don't know," Nana said. "Boys, maybe?"

"We'll never meet any," Cady said gloomily. "Not at Arroyo." The Arroyo School was girls-only.

"Well, but *some*day," Nana said. She drew her knees up to her chest and clasped her arms around them. "I do want to get married someday, don't you?" she asked Cady.

Cady nodded her head. "I guess," she said. "I mean, I want to have children, and I want them to have a regular family, so I guess I'd better get married. But it's funny—I can picture the kids better than I can picture a husband."

"Me too," Nana said. "I want to have three boys."

"Three boys!" Cady said, startled that her friend had imagined things so clearly.

Nana smiled, suddenly shy. "But not right away," she

said. "I don't even want to get *married* right away. First, I want to become a doctor."

Cady nodded, familiar with this plan. Nana had become interested in medicine during the treatment of her illness. "That takes a long time," she said.

"I know, but it'll be worth it," Nana told her. "And I want to date lots of guys before I get married, but I can do that while I'm in med school. It'll be perfect."

"What if you fall in love with one of the med school guys, though?" Cady asked. "Won't that wreck everything?"

Nana shook her head violently. "Nuh-uh. *Nothing* is going to wreck my plan," she said. "If he's the right guy, he can wait until I'm ready to get married."

"Wow," Cady said. "You have it all figured out."

"What about you?" Nana asked. "How many kids do you want to have?"

Cady swallowed some cider, then wiped her mouth on her sleeve. "Oh, I don't know. One or two, I guess. But I want to have *girls*," she added fiercely.

"I don't blame you, after Russell," Nana giggled. Russell was Cady's little brother.

"But let's live close together even when we grow up and get married, okay?" Cady asked. "That way, our kids can be friends, too."

"Okay," Nana said, nodding. "Or else they can drive each other crazy."

"Whatever," Cady said, laughing.

Nana stretched out one of her legs and made a face.

"Is it hurting again?" Cady asked, worry zipping through her like an electric shock.

"A little bit," Nana admitted.

"Well, we better go home. It's time, anyways," Cady said.

Nana reached for the bottle of sparkling cider. "Wait a minute," she said. "I want to make a toast, too."

Cady settled back onto the woolly blanket and waited.

Nana lifted the bottle. "To us," she said. "Best friends forever!"

"Forever," Cady echoed.

And somewhere in the distance, a dog began to bark.

Chapter One

Hoping

━━━━━━━━

"I TOLD YOU BEFORE, I already know how to swim. They taught us in preschool," Russell said. He was five years old, and he sounded pained, as though he was having to explain that he knew how to breathe.

"I'm still supposed to watch you," Cady said, bored. School had ended only a day earlier, but already the California summer seemed weeks old. Sunshine, smog, and chlorine. And then there was sunburn. "Keep your T-shirt on, Russ," she reminded her little brother as he inched sideways down the black-and-white-tiled steps into the water. He stopped trying to remove his shirt and gripped the shiny railing again with both hands.

"But how am I ever going to get a tan if I keep my shirt on?" he complained.

"You have red hair. You don't *get* tan, Russell," Cady said. "You get blisters and have to go to the doctor, remember?"

"Just that one time," Russell said, going down another step. The white T-shirt ballooned around his narrow middle like a jellyfish. "And how come you never get blisters, anyway? That's no fair!"

Cady sighed, wishing she had brought a library book with her to her neighbors' swimming pool. She didn't feel like swimming today. Instead, she was trying out her new white shorts for the first time.

The Morgans were generous with their pool. Selected neighbors could thread their way down the steep shady path at the side of their house to use it when they wanted. Kids had to be invited, though, as Cady and Russell had been. All that people swimming at the Morgans' house had to do was close the gate behind them, use the buddy system, and pick up after themselves. "I don't burn, I have brown hair, remember?" she said to her brother.

"Yeah, but so what?" Russell said. Now he was standing in the shallow end. He reached his hand out for the side of the pool and bunny-hopped his way over to it. "It's freezing in here," he complained.

"Mmm," Cady said. She was thinking about Nana.

"I can swim really far," Russell said. "They taught me." He sounded as though he was announcing something to himself.

"That's good," Cady said automatically. She didn't think he'd really learned how to swim in preschool, but who could tell? All his friends had learned when they were babies, practically, but earaches had kept Russell out of the water most summers.

"Cady, watch this!" Russell said, and he started bouncing up and down in the water. His T-shirt clung to him in shiny white folds, and his skin gleamed pink through the white cotton.

"Make sure you hold on to the side, Russ," Cady said.

"Bouncy, bouncy," Russell sang under his breath.

Cady thought about the last day of school. Sixth grade was finally over. Thank goodness, she thought. Not that things had been so bad—until April, anyway.

That's when Nana had started staying home from school.

"Watch me," Russell shouted. There were longer intervals between his bounces now, which meant he was in deeper water, Cady realized suddenly.

"Russell, get—"

"Bouncy, bouncy, BOUNCE!" Russell shot up into the air. His hands pulled clear of the pool's edge, and when he came back down he was flailing in the water.

And he was in over his head.

Cady jumped to her feet, sure that in one second he would recover and start dog-paddling his way to safety. He could dog-paddle at least, couldn't he?

Two seconds later, Cady was in the water, brand-new shorts and all.

Ten seconds later, Russell was safe. Coughing, sputtering, but safe. "Russell, for crying out loud!" Cady shouted, her heart pounding. One hand still gripped her little brother's flimsy white shirt. She could see his ribs heave as he gasped for breath. "Are you okay?"

"I'm—I'm—"

"Don't talk, *breathe,*" she ordered him.

Russell shuddered and dragged in raspy lungfuls of air. "*Gah,*" he said.

"You scared me to death," Cady scolded, clutching him against her suddenly.

"Then how come you're yelling at me?" he asked, and he started to cry.

"I don't know!" Cady said, shaking him a little. "How come you told me you could swim?"

"I don't know," Russell said, echoing her. "I thought I could," he added, looking a little lost. "It's no fair that I'm the only kid in Pasadena who can't swim. So the minute I said I could, I thought it was true." He pulled away from Cady. "You look weird," he said, suddenly solemn. "And I can see through your shorts, almost."

Cady glared at him past her dripping bangs and pulled the white shorts away from her legs. Her sneakers were sodden, and her shirt was sticking to her skin. And she was going to have to walk home like this! "Well, it doesn't matter if it's no fair that you can't swim, Russ," Cady said, exasperated. "You don't know how yet."

"I know," Russell said.

But he still didn't look entirely convinced.

• • •

"I'm feeling better, really," Nana Weber assured her mom the next morning.

"We'll go slow, Mrs. Weber," Cady promised. "I'll take care of her, don't worry." Cady had always been the careful one—compared to her best friend, Nana, former daredevil, anyway.

"And Dr. Pig said I'm supposed to get some exercise, to build up my strength," Nana said.

"It's Dr. *Pogue*," her mother corrected automatically.

"I like 'Pig' better," Nana said. "Anyway, he's my doctor. I can call him what I want." She was starting to get grouchy; Cady had noticed that this was happening a lot lately.

"Well," Mrs. Weber said, making a bright, determined effort to change the subject, "I don't suppose a little walk would hurt. Not if you remember to take it easy." Her soft voice had its usual everything's-going-to-be-okay tone, but her blue eyes were wide with worry. She looked at Cady like a spaniel begging for a biscuit.

"We'll take it easy as pie," Cady assured her. Nana didn't say anything. Instead, she made an impatient little noise, took Cady's arm, and pulled her down the hall.

"Just don't overdo things," Mrs. Weber called after them. "Don't forget that you have to walk all the way back, once you get there."

"I think I could have figured that out, *Mom*," Nana said. She was *definitely* getting grouchy.

"We better leave before it gets too hot out," Cady said, trying to get Nana away from the house before a fight started.

Nana's fights with her mother were becoming famous in the neighborhood.

Nana's mother looked anxious as the two girls neared the front door. "Well, but don't forget—"

"To breathe in, then breathe out," Nana muttered.

"We won't forget," Cady said over her shoulder.

Cady and Nana hurried away from the Webers' house and started up Pine Crest Road. But the road was steep, and pretty soon they were walking slowly—so slowly, in fact, that Cady was secretly shocked. Was Nana really that weak now? This hill was usually nothing to them!

"I'm sorry I'm so slow," Nana said, as if reading Cady's mind. "Pig said it was going to *take some time* before I felt stronger." She sounded as though she was quoting the famous Dr. Pogue as she stressed the words.

"But he thinks the radiation is really going to help?"

"For a while, anyway. If it helps my leg bone, I'll be more *comfortable*," she added, as if finishing another of Dr. Pig's quotations. Increased fatigue and leg pain in April, and a follow-up bone scan in May, had revealed that Nana's cancer had spread further and faster than anyone had realized.

"But does your leg hurt now?" Cady asked. Nana never complained much, not even to Cady.

She had always been like that, Cady remembered. Even in preschool, Nana would roar around on a Big Wheel, unafraid of the bigger, rougher kids, and then act as if nothing had happened when she got smashed up.

Cady, on the other hand, had been afraid even to go down the slide. Nana had finally climbed up the ladder one morning when Cady was standing frozen at the top of the slide, had managed to crawl in front of her friend, and then had inched her way down the steep ramp with Cady seemingly glued to her back.

"I guess my leg aches a little," Nana admitted. "But it's not too bad. Better than before," she added. "So maybe it was worth it."

"Did the radiation hurt—while they were doing it?" Cady persisted. She couldn't picture the treatment.

They were slowly—s-l-o-w-l-y—passing the Morgans' house, scene of Russell's famous swim.

"Nuh-uh," Nana said, shaking her head. Her short black curls bounced a little. "I mean it's hard, because you have to hold so still. And they mark you all up with permanent ink, like you're this science project or something."

"How come?"

"So they know exactly where to zap you," Nana said, narrowing her brown eyes when she said the word *zap*. "But I just pretended I was getting a tattoo," she said with a grin. "A dragon. No," she continued, "it's not as bad as chemo, anyway." She patted her hair, which had finally grown back following a difficult round of chemotherapy eighteen months before.

"Huh," Cady said.

"The radiation hurts about as much as getting your picture taken," Nana continued, "but you can feel kind of crummy afterwards. Like the way I feel now, for instance," she said, trying to act casual as she paused to catch her breath. She pretended to look at the view, but there wasn't much to see—not yet. They still had a ways to go.

"Do you want to go back home?" Cady asked her friend. "We can always walk up to the lot some other day." She thought again of the vacant lot at the top of the hill. It was one of their favorite places, the highest spot on Pine Crest Road and the only empty space left in the entire neighborhood. And they hadn't been up there since Nana's birthday.

"No, I want to keep on going," Nana said stubbornly. "I want to see if it's still for sale."

Cady pretended she was a fortune-teller. She shut her eyes and waved her hands around in front of her. "I predict that...it is," she said dramatically.

"Hey, take a risk while you're at it," Nana said, laughing a little. "Like that lot hasn't been on the market for five months already." Nana had had big plans for the property from the moment she'd seen it; she wanted to buy the lot someday and then keep it perfectly empty and wild.

The girls plodded a little further up Pine Crest. Although it wasn't even nine o'clock in the morning, the temperature was eighty degrees. It was going to be over one hundred again, the fourth day in a row. A bright blue scrub jay landed on a nearby plant and squawked at some invisible enemy.

"That's called Yesterday, Today, and Tomorrow," Nana said, stopping again.

"What is?"

"That plant. See the flowers on it? They change colors after they open. The colors are different yesterday, today, and tomorrow. Purple, lavender, and white for tomorrow. My mom taught me that—she's good at flowers. But I'm still not sure it's going to help."

"Huh?" Cady asked, confused. "You're not sure *what's* going to help?"

"The radiation. I still might die."

Die! Cady's heart seemed to skitter in her chest. "Well, everyone is going to die," she said, trying to sound calm and teacherlike as she said the word. "Hey," she added, attempting a gloomy old joke of theirs, "Who knows who will go first? I could get hit by that bus people keep talking about."

For years, the girls had giggled about it—how grownups seemed always to finish a conversation about doing something dangerous by saying, *Yeah, but of course you could always get hit by a bus. . . .*

"But you probably won't," Nana said flatly, without even the tiniest smile on her face. "And you know it, too," she added. They were finally approaching the vacant lot.

"I guess," Cady admitted. It was strange, she thought, but she felt almost...*embarrassed* that they were having this conversation. And she was embarrassed that she felt embarrassed.

Nana bit her lower lip.

"But I don't get it!" Cady said, her anger suddenly bubbling up. "I thought they were making all these medical discoveries nowadays. Lots of people get cancer, and *they* do okay. Especially kids! And there are people who get over it completely. Why not you?"

"Well," Nana said, "it's just *not* me who's getting better, that's all. At least not very fast. Not fast enough. And some kids do die, you know, Cady."

"Oh, Nan, I know. It's just that—"

"You're getting to be as bad as my mom and dad," Nana interrupted, scowling. "It's like I have to pretend everything's going okay just to make *them* feel good. When they know perfectly well—"

"I guess they have to keep their hopes up," Cady interrupted. Did Nana *have* to keep talking about this?

"Well, yeah, but now Mom's all, 'Oh, be careful, or you won't get better!' So it will be all my fault when the next thing goes wrong, which it *might.* But I guess then it will be easier for her," Nana finished. She kicked viciously at a eucalyptus nut.

Cady took a deep breath and tried again. "Maybe your mom is just hoping—"

"Of course she's *hoping,*" Nana said. "But she's also making it so I can't even talk to her! You know, about real things. Stuff that I'm scared might happen. Stuff that *could* happen."

"I guess maybe she just wants everything to work out all right," Cady said. Instantly, the words *all right* sounded all wrong to her.

And they reminded her suddenly of the time—just last year, although it seemed far longer ago now—when a fast-served tennis ball had hit her in the neck during a group lesson. She had dropped to her knees on the court, stunned.

And when the stuck-up tennis pro had smoothed his

hair back and called out, "Oh, you'll be all right," a furious Nana—still fuzz-headed from chemo—had raced across two courts to Cady's side and stood over her, trembling.

"She is *not* all right!" Nana had cried out, hands on her hips.

Everyone's jaw had dropped, Cady remembered, including hers—and the tennis pro's. He had apologized on the spot.

"Hey, we're here. We made it," Nana announced. The two friends looked around.

Almost all of the spring wildflowers on the hill had wilted and died in the first blast of summer heat. They looked as though they would crunch if you stepped on them, though a mat of dried pine needles underneath cushioned the girls' steps. Cady picked a dandelion and stuck it behind her ear—a crayon-yellow flower against light brown hair.

But the FOR SALE sign was still up. "Thank goodness," Nana said, brushing some grit off it. She looked down at her dirty fingers and frowned. "I just know some rich guy is going to buy this lot and build a big old monster house on it. Then he'll hog the whole view for himself."

As if summoned by magic, a dark green car came around the corner and slowed down as it neared the vacant lot. "I wonder what *he* wants," Cady said.

"Quick," Nana ordered. "Stand in front of the sign!" Cady and Nana linked arms and stood side by side, blocking the FOR SALE sign from view. They tried to look as though they belonged there—were *planted* there.

"What if he stops the car and gets out?" Cady whispered.

"We'll tell him it's already sold," Nana whispered back. But the car didn't stop.

Cady and Nana turned and looked out over the dried grasses. The lot faced west; scattered houses turned into neighborhoods, and neighborhoods blended into the distant towers of downtown Los Angeles. Beyond that, some days you could even see a low, far-off silver gleam that was the Pacific Ocean; never when it was this smoggy, though.

Cady felt her muscles trying to relax; they ached almost the same as when she'd had the flu. Which was funny, she thought—because *she* wasn't the one who was sick.

Nana was.

Boy, was she ever.

Sick! The very word sounded like something breaking, Cady thought, or like a lock clicking in a door. It was a terrible word, but illness wasn't going to change a thing between her and Nana. *They,* at least, would be able to talk about real things—the *realest* things, Cady thought—always, no matter what.

Behind her back, though, Cady crossed her fingers.

• • •

Three weeks later, Nana's condition was worse, but strangely, Cady had never felt more alive. "I don't know, Nan," she said, sitting in the Webers' living room. "I feel kind of guilty, like I'm this vampire or something. I mean I walk up to your house, then da-da-da-da-*dah,* and when I leave I feel great!"

"Why?" Nana asked. "Because you don't have to hang around with me anymore that day?" She was resting almost all the time now.

"Oh, come on. Like I want to go sit alone in my boiling-hot room all summer," Cady joked, "or even better, take care of Russell." She had been seeing other friends, too, but Nana seemed to get irritated hearing about them. So Cady had learned to keep her mouth shut.

Nana didn't mind hearing about Russell, though; she thought he was funny. Of course, Cady mused, that was probably because she was an only child. Nana's parents had always said that one Nana was plenty.

"I could always take Russell swimming at the Morgans' again," Cady said. "That would be *loads* of fun." The two friends grinned at each other, thinking of Cady's feisty little brother.

"Well," Nana said, "what do you mean, then, about feeling so great when you leave? Do you mean you feel good because you're not the one who has cancer?"

Cady pointed a toe, inspecting her tan. Nana's was even darker; she spent a lot of time lately lying on a lawn chair out on the long wooden deck that overlooked a steep, tree-packed slope. Beyond lay Pasadena's Arroyo Seco, the dry arroyo, and—somewhere behind the summer smog— the San Gabriel Mountains. "No," she said slowly, "not exactly. It's not so much what I *don't* have. I guess maybe I just appreciate things more. Like, oh, I don't know—like my feet, say."

"Oh, well, your *feet,*" Nana said, as if that explained everything.

Cady laughed. "Well, not the actual feet, maybe," she said. "It's more what they can do. Like walking and stuff."

Except that really pointed out how unfair things were, Cady thought suddenly. When she had walked, Nana had run—or skated, or danced, or ridden her bike. The old Nana had enough energy for *two* people. And that's the way it had usually been, Cady thought suddenly; Nana had led the way, and she—Cady—followed, as if towed by a magnet.

"Yeah, walking's good," Nana agreed. She yawned and tucked her own narrow feet under a flowered sofa cushion. "Hey, remember that walk we took a couple of weeks ago?" she asked. She sounded as though she was remembering a long-ago trip to Disneyland.

Cady squinted her green eyes as she looked out the Webers' living room window. A hummingbird feeder shimmered in the sunlight.

"Those were the days, huh?" Nana teased, poking at Cady's knee. "When we could go for a walk? The good old days. Only we just didn't know it yet."

Chapter Two

The Fourth of July

NANA WAS READMITTED TO Wallace Cancer Hospital in the middle of the night on June twenty-seventh. Mr. Weber often had to travel because of business, but he was home that night, and so he and Mrs. Weber drove Nana there.

When Cady came to the Webers' house for a visit early the next morning as planned, Mr. and Mrs. Weber were still asleep. Cady stood on the Webers' doorstep in the morning sunlight, her hair tucked neatly behind her ears, and rang the doorbell a second time. Finally, Mrs. Weber came to the door in her faded pink chenille bathrobe and told Cady what had happened during the night.

Cady shook her head slightly as she heard the news. "But what's wrong with her, exactly?" she asked Mrs. Weber. She tried to keep her face calm and her voice steady so that Nana's mom would tell her the truth, and keep *on* telling her the truth.

Nana's mother stood tall and thin at the front door, clutching the neck of her bathrobe. "Oh, Cady, she—well, she started getting sick, honey. You know. Ill. Violently ill."

Nana had been *vomiting,* Cady thought angrily. Why couldn't Mrs. Weber just say the word?

"She'll be in the hospital for a couple of days, only until she gets back to normal," Mrs. Weber said.

Whatever that means, Cady thought. She glared at Mrs. Weber's bathrobe sash, which had come untied and trailed on the floor. It looked helpless, somehow, and shabby, Cady thought.

When she called the hospital later that day, Cady told Nana, "We've got to get you out of there. Oh, I wish I could drive!" She sounded a lot braver than she was feeling.

Anyway, Nana was usually the one who had rescued *her*—like on the tennis court, or like that terrible time in third grade when they had gone ice skating together. Cady had clung to the railing like Magnet Girl, she remembered, her ankles suddenly boneless. Nana was a slightly better skater and had kept her company for a while, inching along the edge of the rink. But then she had gone for a quick dash across the ice to get warm.

That's when a laughing mob of big sixth-grade boys had pulled Cady to the center of the rink—and abandoned her there! Nana had skate-stumbled to her side, cheeks blazing pink with exertion and indignation. She and a tear-spattered Cady had ended up crawling back to the side of the rink on their icy hands and knees.

And obviously Nana could have skated the distance.

But best of all was their revenge on the boys, who—off the ice—had left their snacks unattended while they were tormenting some other little kid. Cady and Nana swooped by the snack counter themselves, and then, armed with packets of sugar and salt, they spiced up the boys' treats. Sugar on the nachos, salt in the Cokes, Cady remembered. She sighed.

Nana said, "It's okay, don't feel bad, Cady. I feel safer in the hospital. I was so scared last night!"

Who *is* this person? Cady wondered, hanging up the phone.

• • •

Dr. Pig wouldn't say when Nana could come home. Nana seemed to get weaker day by day despite the fluid that seeped from the clear plastic bag, down a long tube, and through the tiny needle in her wrist. Nana said the needle didn't hurt at all, really—only she couldn't move around easily, all hooked up like that.

Not that she was going anywhere.

• • •

Cady dangled her feet in the cool water of the Morgans' swimming pool. It was the morning of July fourth, and she was supposed to be watching Russell while he splashed around, or *swam,* as he put it. After what had happened last time, Cady was afraid even to blink.

She glanced over at him; skinny, red-haired Russell was holding on to the side of the pool again, bouncing in place. He was singing under his breath: "It's the Fourth of July, it's the Fourth of July. BLAM!" With each "blam," Russell smashed one of his fists into the water. At least he was being cautious today.

Cady sighed and sneaked a look at her watery feet again. The pool made them appear to be cut off from the rest of her body. It was like watching herself on TV, Cady thought. She wriggled all ten toes to make sure they were really hers.

"Penny for your thoughts!" Mrs. Morgan whispered in Cady's ear.

Cady jumped a little. Mrs. Morgan was always

sneaking up that way, she thought, embarrassed. The Morgans' pool was on a lower level than their house—most of the properties on hilly Pine Crest were like that, on different levels—which meant that anyone approaching should have made some noise. Especially when they were wearing flip-flops with huge plastic flowers on them. "Oh, hi, Mrs. Morgan," Cady said. "Thanks for inviting us over to swim."

Mrs. Morgan smiled, kicked off her flip-flops with a flourish, and sat down next to Cady—as though she were just a kid who had never grown up. But Mrs. Morgan was like that. She and her husband didn't have children of their own; in fact, real little kids seemed to make them nervous.

When he wasn't working, Mr. Morgan was either playing tennis, fiddling with his sound system, or getting ready to go rock climbing. He never seemed to sit still for a second.

Cady's dad, on the other hand, liked nothing better than to stretch out and listen to music or read a book. But maybe that was because he spent all day, every day, preparing buildings for earthquakes. Maybe that made him nervous; he probably just needed more rest than Mr. Morgan, Cady thought.

Like her husband, Mrs. Morgan was always running around, usually in a tennis dress, which made her look like an overgrown toddler. She wore little white socks with pink pompons at the heels. In the summer she often padded around the yard in her bathing suit, pulling on a pair of shorts and a T-shirt whenever she had to go out. She looked ready for day camp then. It always startled Cady for a second to see Mrs. Morgan driving a car; how could a little kid like that drive?

But she usually didn't have to speak with the woman.

"BLAM!" Russell sang out.

"Keep it down, Russ," Cady instructed him.

"Do you think your brother might be having a problem with—with violence, hon?" Mrs. Morgan asked, her voice low, confidential.

"Who, Russell?" Cady smiled a little, imagining her brother as he saved ants from the sprinkler, sang lullabies to his turtles, or pretended he was the daddy with his stuffed animals. "No, he's okay," she assured her neighbor.

"I hope so," Mrs. Morgan said, not sounding convinced.

"Are you and Mr. Morgan going to the picnic and fireworks this year?" Cady asked, trying to change the subject. Several Pine Crest families had gotten into the habit of picnicking together at nearby Mission Park each July fourth, then staying to watch the fireworks display.

"Sure," Mrs. Morgan said, kicking her freckled legs playfully in the water. A silvery arc of water caught the sunlight. "Aren't you guys?"

"I guess so, sure," Cady said. In fact, Cady's mom and dad were taking only Russell this year. Cady had gotten permission to go visit Nana at the hospital. Mrs. Weber was going to give her a ride. She didn't want to explain this to Mrs. Morgan, though.

"Is that poor little Nana Weber still over at the cancer hospital?" Mrs. Morgan asked, as if reading Cady's mind.

"Well, yes, but it's just for a few days," Cady said. "It's nothing serious." Mrs. Morgan looked at Cady pityingly. "No, *really*," Cady went on. Suddenly it seemed as though it was the most important thing in the world to convince Mrs. Morgan that Nana was going to be okay. "She just needed some extra fluids, that's all. She—I guess she got kind of weak at home. For some reason. Maybe she caught a little bug."

"Her poor mother and father," Mrs. Morgan said with a dramatic sigh. "My heart goes out to them." She clutched at the front of her bathing suit as if ready to demonstrate this.

Cady thought about Mr. and Mrs. Weber. Nana's dad had always been gone a lot, but lately he seemed to be away even more. When he was around, he acted the way he usually did—a big, red-faced man, he was possibly a little more jokey than before, even.

Nana's mother was quieter, and worried, of course. But she had always been a worrier. Cady used to think this was because Nana was an only child. Mrs. Weber had often acted as though the worst thing that could happen *would* happen. When the girls had gone horseback riding, for instance, Mrs. Weber warned them, "Don't take off your riding hats, even for a second. If a horse rears, you could end up in a coma—or *worse*." Whenever Cady and Nana had gone out for a walk, Mrs. Weber would say, "Keep an eye out for drunk drivers, especially coming around corners. Promise?"

Well, maybe Mrs. Weber was right after all, Cady thought now. The worst thing *had* happened. Maybe Nana's mother was almost relieved to get it over with!

Cady didn't say anything to Mrs. Morgan, though. Nana and her problems were none of this woman's business.

Mrs. Morgan persisted. "But you think Nana's coming home pretty soon?"

"Mmm," Cady said, nodding her head *yes*.

"Cady, watch this!" Russell shouted. "BLAM!" He let

go of the pool's side and hit the sparkling water with both fists.

"Goodness!" Mrs. Morgan said, holding up her hands as if protecting her face from invisible rays. "Is he pretending he has some kind of weapon?"

"Russell," Cady called, struggling to her feet, "get out and dry off. We have to go home."

"Already?" he cried, outraged. "But I'm not even wrinkly yet. And it's the Fourth of July!"

"Out, Russell. You promised, no hassles this time. Remember?"

"Oh, okay," he said, pouting. But he got out.

• • •

Cady and Russell walked down Pine Crest Road, heading home. They lived three houses down the hill from Nana's house. Mrs. Weber was in her driveway, putting a pile of books into her dark blue station wagon. Her tall thin body bent over the backseat like a flex-straw. Someone had printed WASH ME! in the dust on the side of the car. That was pretty harsh, Cady thought. But after all, the person who did it couldn't have known about Nana. "Hi, Cady, and Russell darling," Mrs. Weber called out, straightening up.

Cady heard Russell hiss under his breath; he hated being called *darling* as much as Cady hated being called *hon*. "Hi, Mrs. Weber," Cady said.

"Don't forget about tonight, Cady. Pick you up at around six-thirty?"

"Okay, I'll be ready," Cady said.

"I'm packing a picnic basket and everything. You girls can watch the fireworks from Nana's window."

"Okay," Cady repeated.

"You and Russell be careful walking around that corner, now. I've seen cars come whizzing—"

"Okay," Cady called over her shoulder. She was trotting now to keep up with her little brother. Usually, Mrs. Weber's suggestions—repeated almost as a worried chant—got on her nerves. Today, though, the woman's reminders seemed, as Cady had been saying repeatedly just now, *okay.*

• • •

"But how come we had to leave so fast?" Russell asked, slamming the Wintons' heavy front door behind him. He was still angry about getting out of the pool.

"Put your towel in the hamper," Cady said, seconds before he threw it down on the big square tiles of the hall floor.

"You expect me to do *everything,*" he said bitterly. "First I have to get out of the swimming pool, and now you want me to put the towel in the hamper."

"Are you hungry for lunch yet?" Cady asked, hoping to distract him before he got any crankier.

"And anyway, how come you're not coming with us tonight?" Russell demanded, ignoring his sister's question. His blue eyes glared at Cady. "You always go with us. It's a family *tradition.*"

Cady laughed. "I didn't think you knew what that word meant."

"Everybody knows what it means," he said, scornful. "It means you have to do it, no matter what. Even if you don't feel like it! Even you, Cady. Just because you're twelve, that doesn't mean—"

Cady interrupted him: "Well, traditions were made to be broken, I guess," she said airily.

Russell looked shocked at this. Then he recovered and tried a new argument. "But you're always over at Nana's. You're never home anymore."

"Nana's in the hospital, Russ."

"She's *always* in the hospital!"

"No, she isn't. She—"

"Yes, she is too," Russell interrupted. "In the hospital, or sick in bed. It's boring! She's wrecking all our fun. Why doesn't she just get better, anyway?"

"Because she can't, that's why." Cady seemed to hear another door slam shut as she said these words.

"She could if she wanted to," Russell said, hands on his skinny little hips. "And anyways, even Daddy says you spend too much time visiting her," he added, sounding important.

Cady couldn't believe what she was hearing. "Daddy says—when did he say that?"

"He told Mommy. I *heard* him."

"So you were spying on them?"

"No, it was an accident," Russell said, prim all of a sudden.

Cady spotted some little white goose bumps on Russell's spindly sunburned arms. It looked as though there was one bump for each freckle there. "Better go get dressed, Mr. Big Ears, before you catch a cold," she said.

"Even if I did catch a cold and had to go to the hospital you wouldn't come see me," Russell said. "You'd be all busy with Na-Na-Na-Nanny Goat." He trotted off down the hall, happy to have had the last word.

• • •

A key sounded in the lock, and the front door swung open. "Well, we're back from our famous annual Fourth of July walk around the neighborhood," Cady's mother announced grimly.

Cady's dad always referred to this walk as the Grand Tour. He said it marked the official start of summer. "It was great," he said enthusiastically, tugging at his new shorts. Mr. Winton's face was tan—pink from the walk, really—but his bare legs still looked winter-pale, as if they'd been carved from a bar of Ivory soap.

"It was great if you don't count getting stalked by a barking, slavering dog, John," Cady's mother said, looking up at her husband. "You know Moxie Lewis," she asked Cady, "who's always running around loose?" She and her husband wandered into the kitchen as they talked, and Cady followed, stiff-legged.

"Oh, I'm sure Moxie has had his rabies shot," Mr. Winton said. "At least he wasn't actually frothing at the mouth."

Cady listened to her parents; they sounded far away, or as if they were on the other side of a sliding glass door.

Did they really think that she was spending too much time with Nana? With her very best friend, who needed her?

"Well," Cady's mother said, pouring herself a glass of water, "there's such a thing as a leash law in this town. And you and I ought to be able to take one lousy walk together a year without being threatened by some lunatic dachshund. Which reminds me, where's Russell?" Cady knew that Mrs. Winton didn't really mean the pesky dog was in any way like Russell. But her son—who was allergic to furry animals—had wanted a dog most of his life. It had been a noisy, ongoing campaign. He had three little turtles instead.

"He's changing his clothes," Cady said. "He's all mad because I made him get out of the pool too soon. According to *him*."

"Why'd you make him get out?" her father wanted to know. He rinsed a bunch of grapes and started nipping them off, one by one, as he leaned over the sink. Mr. Winton was an enthusiastic eater.

"Oh, that goofy Mrs. Morgan came out and started bothering me. Talking and everything," Cady finished, her voice trailing off.

"Well, it *is* her pool," Mrs. Winton said, frowning a little. "But I must admit I know what you mean. She can talk up a storm. Maybe I'd better go check on Russell. Make sure he doesn't put on anything weird."

"I'll go," Cady said, sounding a little too eager.

"Try to get him to wear that new pair of shorts I bought him," her mother said. She tucked her red polo shirt neatly into her own cuffed white shorts as she spoke.

"Better give it up, Mom. He's never going to put those on," Cady said. Russell could be extremely stubborn about the most unexpected things—and wearing shorts was apparently going to be one of them.

"Tell him Daddy's wearing *his* new shorts," Mrs. Winton called out as Cady headed down the hall.

"Oh, that ought to do it," her husband said gloomily, casting a comic look down at his pale legs. "Poor kid," he added.

• • •

"Hey, Russ," Cady said. Her brother—dressed in his underpants and a faded Dodgers T-shirt—was sitting cross-legged on the striped rug in his room. Another stripe, of sunlight, spilled across his legs.

Russell was lining up pale wooden blocks along the rug's pattern. "I'm busy," he announced.

"What are you doing?" Cady sat down next to him.

"Building a racetrack for my turtles. It's special, for the Fourth of July," he added. "Want to help?" Cady could tell he was starting to forget about being mad.

"Sure," Cady said, reaching for a block. "Who's going to win, do you think? Tommy, Joe, or Richard?" Russell had gone through a period where he hated his own name, and he'd given his turtles names he liked better. Plain names, as he put it. He was the only one so far who could tell them apart, though.

"Richard's going to win," her brother said promptly. "But I don't know that for sure," he added, trying to be fair.

"So are we all invited to the big race?" Cady asked.

"Yeah, after lunch," Russell said. He carefully balanced a rectangular block on top of two others, making a bridge. "They're resting up."

Cady glanced over at Russell's terrarium, in which nothing ever seemed to move. "How can you tell?" she asked.

"I just know, okay?" Russell said. "They're my turtles, don't forget."

"Okay, okay," Cady said hastily. "I was just asking, that's all. Hey," she added, "what do you think about putting on those shorts Mom bought you?"

Russell gave her a look. "They're all new and scratchy," he said finally. "I'll wear them when they get old and soft."

"But Russ," Cady said, "they're never going to get old if you don't wear them."

Russell scowled. "You want me to go around with itchy legs just so my shorts can get old?" he asked.

"That's not what I—"

"No way," Russell said decisively, and he reached for another block. "That's just dumb, Cady."

Chapter Three

Fireworks

CADY CAREFULLY SIGNED HER NAME in the hospital's register of visitors that evening. Guests had to sign in every single visit and write down exactly where they were going. The big woman behind the desk recognized Cady; she smiled and handed her a sticky name badge.

"Here ya go, sweetheart," the woman said. She gave Cady a bright, sorry smile.

"Thanks," Cady said.

The badges were a different color each day. Today's badge was outlined with red and had an exploding firecracker at the top. Cady put it crooked on her red sweatshirt; that was the only way she had figured out to say *I don't like this*. Once, she had put her name badge on upside down.

Nana had approved. "I'll turn you into a rebel yet," she said.

Cady followed Mrs. Weber down the hall—which was darker and emptier than usual, now that it was evening—and stared at her own sneakered feet while waiting for the elevator to come. There were two elevators that faced each other; they were waiting for the smaller, square elevator. The larger one was big enough to hold a person lying on a gurney. Cady didn't like that one.

"Now, I've got chicken, potato salad, and Jell-O in

here," Mrs. Weber recited, patting the picnic basket that was hooked over one thin arm. She sounded nervous. "Try to get her to eat some of the Jell-O, anyway, and maybe the potato salad," the woman continued.

"Okay," Cady said dully, shifting the old school backpack she held cradled in her arms.

"I'm going to be in that little waiting room next to the nurses' station, writing letters," Mrs. Weber said. "If you need anything..." Her voice trailed away. Cady leaned against the elevator's carpeted wall and stared at the lighted panel that listed the floors.

The hospital had seven floors. Day patients and surgical patients were treated on the first and second floors. The third floor was for pediatric patients—kids staying at the hospital. The fourth floor was for grownups. The fifth floor was for intensive-care patients—people who were very, very sick. Nana said the doctors did research on the sixth and seventh floors.

"Or you can ring for the nurse if there's an emergency," Mrs. Weber was saying. "I think Amanda's on duty tonight." Cady tried not to think about the possibility of an emergency, but once she did that, it was hard to put it out of her mind. What if—

"I thought maybe we'd head home about nine-thirty," Mrs. Weber said. "The fireworks should be over by then." The big elevator doors slid open at the third floor without making a sound.

"Are you sure we'll be able to even *see* any fireworks?" Cady asked. Fireworks were illegal most places in Southern California because of brushfire danger, but organized fireworks displays—such as the one held each year at Mission Park—were allowed.

"Nana's room has a pretty good view," Mrs. Weber said. "The nurses told me you should be able to see the Dodger Stadium fireworks clear as anything. Hello, Amanda," she said, nodding at a nurse who was holding a phone to her ear.

The pretty nurse looked up, nodded back, and mouthed, "Hi." She waved hello to Cady with two fingers, then she straightened a teddy bear holding a little American flag. It leaned against her telephone.

Cady followed Mrs. Weber to Room 317. Nana still had the room to herself, Cady was relieved to see. "Hey, Nan," she said.

"Hey, Cady," Nana said, smiling. She was sitting almost upright in the electric hospital bed, wearing one of her own white summer nightgowns rather than the usual blue-and-white-patterned gown the hospital provided. Nana's short, springy black hair was tied back from her forehead with a floppy bow of thick red yarn. Amanda's work, Cady suspected.

"Oh, the flowers came," Mrs. Weber said, setting the picnic basket on the long, wheeled table next to Nana's bed. Cady held on to her backpack. Mrs. Weber turned to the colorful arrangement next to the window and fussed with a red-white-and-blue-striped ribbon. She tugged at a bright blue carnation. The color looked weird to Cady, for a flower anyway.

"Thanks, Mom. And thank Daddy, too, okay?"

"He just wishes he could be here, darling. But you know, business . . . " Her voice trailed off again.

Mrs. Weber didn't seem to be finishing too many sentences lately, Cady thought.

"So what did you bring?" Nana asked, looking at the picnic basket.

"Oh, a little of this, a little of that," Mrs. Weber said playfully, opening the basket. She took out a red-and-white-checked tablecloth, shook it open with a snap, and spread it on the wheeled table. The table was narrow, so the cloth hung down long on both sides. "Cady will serve up the picnic goodies," Mrs. Weber continued, sounding a little too cheerful. "I already ate."

Really, she didn't look as though she'd eaten for a week, Cady thought.

"Thanks, Mom," Nana said.

"Then when it gets completely dark out, the fireworks should start. The stadium is over in that direction," Mrs. Weber added, gesturing toward one corner of the big window like a tour guide.

"Okay," Nana said. Cady could tell she wanted her mom to leave the room.

"I'll take care of everything," Cady said. "Don't worry, Mrs. Weber."

"Well," the woman said, hesitating at the door, "if you're sure..."

"We're sure, Mom," Nana said, barely controlling her impatience. "But don't forget, Cady gets to stay until nine-thirty. Just like I was still at home."

"Right," Mrs. Weber said automatically. "But you know where the nurse's call button is, Cady?"

"I'll show her," Nana snapped. "You can go now. Really!"

"All right, darling," Mrs. Weber said hurriedly, and out she went.

• • •

"I'm supposed to try to get you to eat some Jell-O and some potato salad," Cady reported as soon as the big door had swung shut. She pulled the gray curtains that hung from the ceiling, surrounding each bed, until they blocked the door's window. She and Nana had always had a deal: no secrets from each other. Cady refused to conspire behind Nana's back, especially with Mrs. Weber, especially now.

It was still Cady and Nana, together against the world, if necessary.

"Gotcha," Nana said. "But let's eat on the bed. Can you move that tablecloth?"

Cady slid the checked cloth off the wheeled table and flapped it over Nana's pale blue cotton blanket. "Want me to sit *on* the bed or next to it?" she asked her friend.

"On it, just like at home," Nana said. "Only don't jounce too much when you sit down, okay?"

Cady moved the picnic basket to one side of Nana's legs and carefully settled herself cross-legged at the end of the bed. She kept her backpack with her, though. She reached for an eagle-decorated paper plate and passed one to Nana.

"Don't you want to get rid of that thing?" Nana asked, nodding at the battered pack. "What's in it, anyway?"

"Oh, it's a surprise," Cady said, mysterious. She reached for a drumstick, pretending to be interested only in it. She licked her lips like a cartoon character. "Yummy!" she said.

But Nana kept her eyes on the backpack. "A surprise? You're kidding," she said, her eyes sparkling. "For me?"

"Mmm," Cady nodded, her mouth full of chicken. "Just for tonight, though," she added, swallowing. "It's sort of a temporary loan."

"What is it, a library book?" Nana asked.

"Close, very close," Cady said, as if judging a TV quiz show. She wiped her fingers on a star-spangled napkin, unzipped her backpack, and reached inside. "It's...Richard the Swift!" Her hand emerged from the pack. She was holding one of Russell's turtles. He had a tiny flag sticker on his shell in honor of the holiday. The creature waved his legs around in the air as if he was swimming. He blinked, startled by the room's light.

"Oh!" Nana was thrilled. "Now I've got *two* Fourth of July visitors!"

"This one's unofficial, though. I sneaked him in," Cady said proudly. "But he's wearing his identification badge in case he gets caught," she added, pointing to the sticker. She set the turtle down on the tablecloth, and he immediately retreated into his shell. "Entertaining, isn't he?" Cady asked, grinning. She tilted her head as she looked at Nana.

"He's great, Cady," Nana said, poking the turtle gently with her finger. "I can't believe you did this—you're usually so law-abiding."

"I just figured you needed a surprise," Cady said, shrugging as if it were nothing. But it was true; Nana had usually been the one to come up with their adventures.

Like that time in first grade when she had convinced Cady they should cut each other's hair—really, really short. So short, in Cady's case, that a visitor had thought she was a little boy. And Nana had said, "Yes, he's my brother Spanky!"

Or like the time last year when Nana had talked Cady into going on the scariest roller coaster at Magic Mountain. Cady didn't even want to think about *that.*

But people could change, Cady thought. *She* could be adventurous too—if necessary! "Well, smuggling turtles isn't really such a big deal," she said, trying to be modest.

"It's big enough," Nana said. "It's the most fun thing that's happened all day, believe me. Oh—he's coming out." Sure enough, Richard was cautiously poking his wrinkled head out of his shell a fraction of an inch at a time. Then his feet emerged, and he started bumbling his way up the bed toward Nana. His little claws caught on the tablecloth, snagging it.

Tenderly, Nana freed him, and he continued his journey.

"Russell gave me permission to bring him, miracle of miracles," Cady said, opening the plastic container of potato salad. "Richard won the turtle race this afternoon. That's why I called him Richard the Swift. Hey, don't let him fall off the bed, though—that's all we need."

"He could be my roommate, then," Nana said, giggling. She made a turtle pen between her legs and the picnic basket and plopped the startled creature right in the middle. "He could wear a cast on his little webby foot, or something. But I thought Russell was so completely jealous about you visiting me all the time."

"He was," Cady said. "He even called you Na-Na-Na-Nanny Goat again this morning. But I bribed him."

"With what?"

"More time in the Morgans' swimming pool," Cady said, rolling her eyes.

There was a sudden *tap tap tap* on the door, and the privacy curtain whooshed out slightly as the door opened. "Hello?" a voice called out.

It was Amanda, the nurse!

Cady tossed her colorful napkin over Richard the Swift a mere second before Amanda poked her head around the curtain. "Sorry to interrupt your party," Amanda said, "but

Mrs. Weber thought you girls might like some ginger ale."
She held up two glistening cans.

Out of the corner of her eye, Cady saw the star-deco-
rated napkin start to move—slowly, but unmistakably—
across the bed. Nana casually put her hand on the napkin as
Cady jumped up to get the soda. "Oh, thanks," Cady said
loudly. "Thanks a *lot*." She knew that she was about to start
gabbling nonsense.

"That was really nice of you," Nana said, as if reading
Cady's mind. She held her hand down firmly on the
squirming turtle. Cady was glad turtles couldn't yell.

"Well, it was your mother's idea, don't forget,"
Amanda said. She hesitated a moment, then added, "Maybe
I should just check your vitals while I'm here." That meant
taking Nana's temperature and blood pressure, Cady knew.

"Oh," Nana said, "can't it wait until Cady leaves?
Tonight is so special, and the fireworks haven't even started
yet."

"Well—"

"*Please?*" Nana begged.

"Okay," Amanda said. "It *is* Independence Day, after
all. I guess you should get to have a little freedom for once."

"Thanks, Amanda," Nana said.

"Yeah, thanks," Cady echoed fervently.

When the door clicked shut again, the two girls looked
at one another for a second, completely silent, then they
burst out laughing. "Oh, I can't believe it!" Nana finally
managed to say.

Cady whisked the napkin off Richard, who squinted
up at her resentfully and shrank back into his shell. "I was so
sure that nurse was going to look down and see your napkin
strolling away," Cady said. "Then she would have called

security, and poor Richard would have gotten thrown in the slammer, and Russell would never have forgiven me."

"Or forgiven *me*," Nana said happily, then she added, "Na-Na-Na-Nanny Goat, who can't catch a billy goat," in a much quieter voice.

"Mmm? What do you mean?" Cady asked, between mouthfuls of potato salad.

"Oh, you know," Nana said. "That rhyme we used to sing? I guess that's really me now."

"How come you think that? About the billy goat?"

"Well, it's obvious, isn't it?" Nana asked, crumpling her starry napkin into a ball. "Look, Cady," she continued, as if explaining something to a little child, "I'm never going to have even one boyfriend, am I? Much less a whole med school full of them."

"I—you don't know that, Nana. I thought that—"

"Yes, I do too know it," Nana said bitterly. "And I'm never going to get married, or have a baby. Or even drive a car, or graduate from high school—or do a million other things. And it really makes me *mad*."

Cady stared down at the red Jell-O on her plate. It was starting to melt a little; the sticky red juice puddled around a blob of potato salad. It looked pretty gross, she thought.

"Cady, wake up!" Nana said, smiling a little stiffly. "Hey, I didn't mean to wreck everything. I thought we could still talk, and stuff."

"We can," Cady said. "I guess I just—I never thought about all that. I mean, I know how sick you are and every-thing, but—"

"No, you don't," Nana said, settling back against her pillow. "I'm sicker than before, if that's even possible. Or maybe it's just that now we know the whole story, how far it's spread. But that's why I'm better off here in the hospital. They did some more tests, did I tell you?"

"Tests?" Cady said blankly.

"Another bone scan, and another blood scan, and a CT scan. You know, the famous *cat scan?*" Nana tried to smile.

"Oh, yeah," Cady said, grinning weakly. It was another old joke of theirs. They had laughingly decided a *cat scan* probably involved a kitty and a spy glass.

"Well," Nana continued, "one good thing, Dr. Pig said we didn't have to do any more chemo. I hated going through that. It wouldn't have helped this time, he said. And the bone marrow transplant is *definitely* out, thank goodness."

"Thank goodness?" Cady asked, confused. "But I thought—"

"That it would be the last amazing thing the doctors would try? That it would be the one treatment that might let me live a little bit longer, when everything else failed?" Nana said, finishing the sentence for Cady in her most sarcastic voice.

"Well, yeah, sort of," Cady said. "That's what you told me *before.*" She twisted her own napkin, trying to get used to yet another new Nana, the one saying these terrible things—yet who seemed so calm.

"That was before," Nana said. "And I guess it works out that way for a lot of people, but it wouldn't work for me. And it's hard to go through. You have to be shut up in total isolation for six weeks, Cady. I mean, I would have gone along with it, sure—in a minute!—but they won't do it if there's no—"

Cady didn't think she could stand it if Nana actually said the words "no hope" together in the same sentence. So she jumped up and started flipping light switches, trying to darken the room. "I think the fireworks are about to start," she said busily. She glanced over at Nana, who had shut her eyes. That stopped Cady, and she hurried back to the bed. "Nana," she whispered, "I'm sorry."

"Me too," Nana said, without opening her eyes. "It's just that you're the only person I can tell. And if *you* can't listen—" A tear crept down the side of her face.

"I can listen," Cady said. "I'll always try to listen from now on, I promise. No matter what."

She reached across the cluttered blanket and touched Nana's hand. It felt so familiar in many ways; Cady guessed that was from the contact of many years during street-crossings, scary movies, and hand-clasped jumps into the deep end of the Morgans' swimming pool.

But Nana's hand felt a little different, too.

Already.

• • •

The two girls watched the distant fireworks display in silence. Cady remembered all the Fourth of Julys they'd spent together at Mission Park: bouncing in the same playpen at first, then digging together in the sandy playground before the holiday picnic, then, years later, trying to roller-skate around the path that circled the entire park, Nana usually leading the way.

And now here they were in Room 317, watching fireworks while tears slid down their faces.

They're cowboy-hat tears, Cady thought, feeling them dry and tighten on her cheeks. The cords of her beloved old red hat had pulled against her face in exactly the same way.

Strangely enough, she thought, the crying wasn't so bad, but it seemed weird not to hear the muffled *pop-pop* of the fireworks or the *oohs* and *aahs* of a friendly crowd. It was odd not to smell that acrid fireworks smell. This was more like watching a fireworks display on television.

Which would be stupid, Cady thought, sneaking a look at Nana. But at least they were together. For this year, anyway.

Richard the Swift grew bold, poked his snubbed nose out of the shell, and looked around. But that was probably only because the room was dark; perhaps he thought everyone had gone home.

The two friends were still there, though.

Chapter Four

Strangers Come to Stay

——————

CADY DID *NOT* WANT to go away on vacation.

"I can't leave now," she said, not wishing to explain further. Ever since Russell had said that her mom and dad thought she was spending too much time with Nana, Cady felt that she and her parents were fighting a silent, invisible battle over...something.

She couldn't say what, exactly.

"You need a break," her father said. He was alone with Cady; Mrs. Winton had taken Russell to a swimming lesson.

"But I don't *want* a break," Cady told him. "Maybe I could stay over at the Webers' house."

Her father was firm. "The Webers have their hands full as it is, Cady. Listen, honey—two weeks isn't a long time," he said, his expression softening. "Nothing will be changed when you get back, I promise. You need a break," he repeated. "We're worried about you, sweetheart. *We* need a break. As a family." Looking tired, he smoothed his sandy hair back with a big freckled hand.

The words popped into Cady's head as if they'd been projected onto a screen: *Nana's my family now.*

But she couldn't speak them aloud.

"Come *on,* Dad," Cady wheedled instead. "*Please* don't make me go with you guys to the beach. Not this summer!" The thought of losing two weeks with her best friend was impossible—even if she was only able to visit Nana three or four times a week in the hospital, and for less than an hour each time, Cady thought.

"This summer is exactly when you need a little time away from Pasadena," her father said flatly. "Your mother and I both agree."

The helpless look in his eyes reminded Cady of Russell in the Morgans' swimming pool, for some reason.

"I just want to stay right here," she whispered, though they were alone in the house.

"You can't," he whispered back. "I'm sorry, Cady."

• • •

By the time the Wintons got back from Laguna, it was the middle of August. Cady's dad went back to work that very afternoon, but the writing classes her mother taught at a nearby college didn't start for another two weeks.

That was good, Cady thought, tossing everything from her duffel bag into the hamper; maybe her mom could drive her to the hospital to see Nana.

She called the Webers' house to work out the best time for a visit.

"Well, Cady, Nana is about to come *home*—for good," Mrs. Weber said.

Nana's mother sounded like an old lady on the phone, Cady thought, startled. "But—but Nana said she liked the nurses at the hospital," she sputtered. "She said she felt safer there!" Cady was bewildered. Hearing such surprising news was like accidentally skipping two chapters in a book, she thought.

"She changed her mind," Mrs. Weber said faintly.

"But I was only gone for two weeks!" Cady said. "When did she decide that she wanted to come home?"

"Well, you can ask her yourself," Mrs. Weber said. "I'm about to leave for the hospital, if you want to come. But check with your mother first."

"I'll be right over," Cady said.

Check with her mother, *right*—she'd leave her mom a note, that's all, Cady thought.

Anyway, her mother was busy reading a story to Russell.

• • •

"But are you really sure you want to come home now?" Cady asked Nana almost as soon as she walked into Room 317.

"Yeah, I'm sure," Nana said. "Hey, I'm glad you're back, by the way. You're so brown," she added, frowning a little.

Nana's own tan had long since faded. And now, Cady saw, her friend was even thinner than before. It was almost as though she had shrunk. In fact, the only parts of Nana that looked bigger were the bones around her eyes, and— under the cotton blanket—her swollen abdomen and bumpy knees.

Cady forced herself to stop spying on these lumps and bumps and look instead into Nana's eyes. "But—but *why* are you leaving the hospital, Nan?" Cady asked. "Who made you change your mind?"

"Nobody did," Nana said, scowling at Cady. "I just want to come home, that's all. I thought you'd be glad."

"I am, I am," Cady assured her. She felt herself flush with embarrassment, though. *But who is going to take care of you?* she wanted to ask.

"Look, Cady. I changed my mind, all right?" Nana sounded impatient. "Now I want to go home and sleep in my own bed. Well, it will be in a hospital bed—Mom and Dad are renting one. But you know what I mean. I want to look out of my own window, and listen to my music as loud as I want, and eat regular food and stuff."

"Oh, can you eat more now?" Cady asked, eager for some good news. Nana had hardly been eating at all when Cady last saw her. And she certainly didn't *look* as if she was eating a lot now, Cady thought.

"That's not the point," Nana said, avoiding Cady's question. "But I think I *could* eat more if I was at home. There'll be nurses, Cady. Don't worry. Don't be scared."

Scared! As usual, Nana was practically reading Cady's mind. How did she know? Cady wondered, ashamed. "Nurses, like here at the hospital?" she asked aloud.

Nana shook her head. "Nuh-uh, hospice nurses," she said. "Well," she corrected herself, "once a week an RN will come to the house to check on things. That's like the head nurse. She'll be in charge of pain control," she added matter-of-factly.

Cady tried not to flinch at these words.

"But mostly it will be LVNs," Nana continued. "That's another kind of nurse. And then there'll be Mom, of course. She'll do a lot. I don't know about Dad. This is something he just can't fix, so he can barely stand to be around it."

Cady wondered what Nana meant when she said *it.* Did she mean herself?

"But at least Mom's stopped looking for someone to blame about all this," Nana said. "That's a relief. And there's a social worker helping her arrange everything. Hey, I get to ride home in an ambulance. That'll be cool." She looked pleadingly at Cady, as if willing her to agree.

But Cady frowned. There was no mention of Dr. Pig anymore, she noticed. He seemed to have disappeared once he'd run out of so-called *procedures* to try on Nana.

And here was Nana herself, Cady thought—becoming the expert on nurses and ambulances when she should be getting ready for school to start. Seventh grade, their first year of Arroyo's middle school. Lockers, and separate classes for each course. *Finally.* And Nana was going to miss it all!

"But can—um—LVNs take good enough care of you at home?" she asked Nana.

"They can do lots of things, like give me a bath or help me into the wheelchair. Stuff like that."

Cady sighed and looked around the hospital room. "Things look different already. Your room is bare, almost."

"Yeah," Nana said, gazing dreamily at an empty bulletin board. "You wouldn't believe how much stuff there was. Mom's been taking things home a little at a time."

Cady cleared her throat. "So when will you—"

"Tomorrow, around noon or so."

Cady looked at Nana, trying to get it straight in her head: the cancer hospital couldn't do anything more to help Nana, she told herself.

Nana wanted to leave, so she was leaving.

Nana was going home to die, Cady thought, making her mind form the sentence.

And maybe that was a good thing. "Cool," she said, trying to smile.

• • •

A strange woman answered the Webers' front door the next afternoon. The woman wore a nurse's uniform but no cap. She had curly blond hair and wore a tag with the name *Irene* on it.

"Is Nana Weber here?" Cady whispered, feeling foolish. She had probably knocked on this door a million times in her life, and now she had to ask a total stranger if she could see Nana?

"She's just waking up," the woman said in a normal, out-loud voice, and she stepped to one side. "You must be Cady. Hi, I'm Irene." She held out her hand, and Cady shifted the brown paper bag she was holding, feeling clumsy.

"Hi," Cady said, and they shook hands. "Where is Mrs. Weber?"

"She and Mr. Weber went out to buy some groceries."

"Well, I brought something to eat," Cady said, holding up the bag. "But I think maybe it's melting. Should I put it in the fridge?"

"Is it for Nana?" Irene asked.

"Part of it is, but I'm not sure—"

"Well, maybe she'd like a little snack. Let's go ask her."

• • •

"I don't *believe* it," Nana said, licking the small white plastic spoon. "A butterscotch sundae!"

"With whipped cream," Cady added, taking another bite of her own sundae. "But no nuts," she added, glancing at the nurse, who was reading in the corner of Nana's room. "They might be too rough on your stomach."

"But how did you—"

"My mom drove me down to South Pas to pick it up." The girls' favorite ice cream hangout was in South Pasadena.

"Oh, I never thought I'd taste another South Pas sundae," Nana said, taking another small bite of ice cream. She sighed happily as it melted in her mouth.

"I was going to get hot fudge, like you usually order," Cady said, "but I thought butterscotch would be—"

"Healthier?" Nana asked, giggling.

Cady heard the Webers' front door open, and Irene stood up. "That's probably your folks," she said to Nana. "I'll go see if they need any help. Give you two a chance to visit." She left the room, closing the door behind her.

"That was nice of her," Cady said. "Does she ever leave you completely alone?"

"Well, not so far. But it's only been a few hours," Nana said. "I hope she will, though—I can always ring if I need help," she said, pointing at a small brass bell on her bedside table. "It's weird, thinking that I might never get to really be alone again," Nana added, looking down at her sundae. "Someone's always going to be keeping track of my every move."

Cady put down her spoon. "Yeah," she agreed. "That would be kind of creepy. Can't you just tell her that you want to be by yourself now and then?"

"Well, Irene's not the only one who'll be taking care of me."

"Who else will there be?" Cady asked.

"Someone at night, always," Nana said. "Two people—they'll split up the week. Then Irene or someone else during the day. Mom, when no one else is here. Oh, and like I said, the RN will come once a week to check on how I'm doing and to take care of this," she said, raising her right arm a little.

A small bandage covered the spot on her wrist where the needle entered. A thin plastic tube connected the needle to a small box—something like a Walkman—that was attached to the metal railing of Nana's bed with black Velcro straps.

"What *is* it?" Cady asked, looking at the little box.

"It's a machine that controls the pain medicine," Nana said, her voice steady. "It's all locked up, with a secret combination and everything. I get the medicine automatically. Oh—and there's this, too," she added. She held up a push button that was connected to the box by another thin wire.

"What's that?"

"My clicker, in case I need an extra dose and nobody's around."

Cady didn't like to think of Nana being in *any* pain, much less being in pain that needed medicine so special that it had to be locked up.

She didn't know what to say. "Hey," she announced, wanting to change the subject, "I looked up *hospice* in the dictionary, and do you know what it said?"

"No, what?" Nana looked down and stirred her plastic spoon in the puddle of melting ice cream.

"It said something like *Hospice: A place where strangers come to stay*," Cady reported.

"Well," Nana said doubtfully, "I guess maybe that's one definition. It sounds kind of old-fashioned, though. I don't think that's what it means anymore."

"Oh," Cady said, scraping her own spoon against the inside of her empty ice cream cup. "It's an old dictionary—it could be wrong. I mean, who would the strangers be? *You're* not a stranger—this is your own house."

"Maybe all the nurses are the strangers," Nana guessed, half joking.

"I hope they're not *too* strange," Cady said, making a funny face. She tried not to look at what she had started to think of as Nana's pain box: maybe *that* was the stranger—that, and the clicker, and the rented hospital bed.

Or maybe cancer was the stranger, come to stay in Nana's body.

There was a muffled knock on Nana's door, and it opened. Mrs. Weber came into the room, and right away she spotted Nana's ice cream. "Oh, darling, do you think that's wise?" she asked, a frown wrinkling part of her narrow forehead.

"I only ate a little," Nana said. "Anyway, it was *good*," she added defiantly.

"Of course it was good," her mother said. "That's not the point, Nana."

The nurse slipped into the room, holding a mug of steaming tea. "Are you done with that sundae, Nana?" she asked, putting the tea down. Turning to Mrs. Weber, she smiled and said, "It's nice to get some calories in her, isn't it?"

"But they're *empty* calories," Mrs. Weber objected.

Nana turned to Cady. "See," she explained, her voice sarcastic, "my mom is afraid I'm going to get cavities, or get too fat, or even—" she paused and lowered her voice dramatically—"get sick and *die*. All from eating ice cream," she added.

Silent, Irene took the soggy cup from her. Mrs. Weber

looked stunned at what Nana had said. Her hands looked big and helpless clasped together.

"I brought the ice cream, Mrs. Weber," Cady said at last, her heart thudding. "I just thought it would be fun."

"Oh, I certainly didn't mean any criticism of you, Cady dear," Mrs. Weber assured her in a shaking voice. "I only—"

"How's my little sweetie?" a man's voice boomed, approaching from down the hall. Mr. Weber poked his head into Nana's room and beamed at Nana and Cady. He wiggled his bushy eyebrows at them and made a funny face.

"I'm fine, Daddy," Nana said. "Only maybe I'm not so sweet today, I guess," she added. She looked angry, defiant, and sorry—all at the same time.

"Don't kid a kidder," her father said. He walked into the room and bent down to kiss Nana's forehead.

He smelled like outdoors, Cady thought; he smelled like far away.

Nana's mother left the room silently, and Irene settled back into her chair with her mug of tea. She picked up her book. "May I?" Nana's father asked, pointing to the foot of her bed. She nodded, and he perched carefully on the cotton blanket, like a big cartoon rooster trying to hatch a hummingbird egg. "So!" he said brightly. His pink face gleamed with perspiration.

Or maybe it was Nana's mom and dad who were the strangers, Cady thought, staring at him. They sure were acting weird, anyway.

"So," Nana said, as if continuing his sentence, "what's new, Daddy?"

"What's new, what's new?" he asked himself, raising his eyes to look at the ceiling. He tapped his chin and squinted a little, as if wondering why the glow-in-the-dark stars, left over from when Nana was a little girl, were still stuck up there. "Oh, I know," he said brightly. "Neighborhood news—the Morgans are getting another car."

"What's so new about that?" Nana teased him. "The Morgans are *always* getting another car."

"True, true," her father admitted with a dramatic sigh.

"Cady has this theory they can't decide on a color they like," Nana said.

"Could be," Mr. Weber said, pretending to consider this. Then he brightened. "Oh, here's another news flash that will cheer you up for sure—the vacant lot up the street finally has a SOLD sign on it."

Nana stared at her father, horrified. "What vacant lot?" she finally asked.

"You know, the one at the top of the hill. About time, too—I thought it was never going to sell, and that hurts everyone's property value."

"But, but—"

"Are you sure?" Cady interrupted. Mr. Weber didn't seem to know anything about Nana, she thought, disgusted. Not a thing!

"Am I sure there's a SOLD sign up?" he asked, confused. "Sure, I'm sure. Why?"

"Oh, we kind of liked the lot empty," Cady said, trying to get an explanation in before Nana exploded.

"Empty?" Mr. Weber said, astounded. "A valuable site like that, going to waste? No way."

"But—but it wasn't going to waste," Nana sputtered.

"Sure it was, honey," her father said, his voice reasonable. Then, as if suddenly realizing Nana's consternation, he softened his voice and added, "Hey, don't let it get to you.

The one sure thing you can count on is change, remember? And just wait—it'll be fun, you'll see."

"What will be fun?" Nana asked, outraged.

"Watching it all happen," her father answered. "You know, watching the house go up. It'll be fun!" he repeated.

Chapter Five

The Real Nana

SCHOOL WAS ABOUT TO START. It was September, and it was hot—hotter than it had been all summer. But that was normal for Southern California. It didn't bother Cady.

What *did* bother her was that Nana wouldn't be going back to school this year. Always before, the two girls had spent the first week of September in nervous but happy preparation for the first day of school. While they didn't need to worry about what to wear, since Arroyo School required its students to wear uniforms, there were always plenty of things to talk about.

For instance, what would the new girls be like? There were always a few, and a couple of them would be both full of their pre-Arroyo adventures and eager to fight the traditions of a new school. That was always entertaining.

And what about the teachers? Would Ms. Sanderson be celebrating the fifth year of her engagement to the hunky guy who sometimes showed up at special school events, or would she finally have gotten married to him?

And then there had been the careful shopping—for new notebooks, dividers, pencils, pens. Cady and Nana had always made a big thing out of that. It seemed as though choosing the right school supplies might affect your luck for the entire year. "I'm going for the whole seventies look," Nana had said last year, selecting lime green and magenta pens and a shiny vinyl notebook. Cady had decided to stick with her usual plain blue canvas notebook. Why mess with a classic?

But *now* what, Cady wondered. Nana wasn't at all interested in talking about the approaching school year.

"Good news," Nana was saying. "I spent an hour sitting up in the wheelchair this morning. I even tried standing for a couple of minutes! Of course, Irene was holding me. Oh, and Irene and I went out on the deck for a while. Maybe tomorrow I can—"

"I'm going to give you a bath tomorrow morning, don't forget," Irene said. Nana was bathed in bed now, but Cady could tell how tiring it was for her. On bath mornings Nana couldn't do anything else until after lunch.

"That's great about the wheelchair," Cady said as Irene left the room.

I guess it's great, she added to herself. But really, what was so wonderful about sitting in a wheelchair? Or about standing up, with someone holding you? Or about going ten inches outside?

Where was Nana, the *real* Nana, who had been able to do almost anything she'd put her mind to—and as recently as last winter? Cady and Nana had ridden horseback, gone skiing, hiked. They'd stayed up at night on weekends, watching videos, eating popcorn, and talking.

One night Nana had decided they should hold the First Annual Batman Film Festival, and they had watched all the Batman movies they could find at the video store back-to-back. And then right before falling asleep, they'd held a Cat-woman competition. Nana awarded Cady first prize when she said the *Mmm, I feel so much yummier!* line so exactly right that they both collapsed, helpless with laughter.

"See, that's the thing about you, Cady," Nana had said, gasping for air. "You go along just as innocent as anything, but then you win the Catwoman prize."

"Hey, what *is* the Catwoman prize?" Cady asked.

"A tuna sandwich. I'll fix you one for breakfast," Nana said. But then they had slept late, late, late, and they'd skipped breakfast.

They hadn't even *heard* of stupid Irene back then, Cady thought now.

Was this Nana even the same person?

• • •

"So what's new with you?" Nana finally asked. Cady sat next to the bed, her bare legs dangling over the arm of the wooden chair. "Been swimming, I see," Nana noted. Cady was wearing her bathing suit, a little stretched, frayed, and bleached now, at the end of a long summer. White elastic threads poked out of the fabric in a few places. The suit reeked of chlorine. Cady had pulled a pair of white shorts on over it.

"Yeah," Cady said. "With Russell, at the Morgans'. Big whoop."

"How *is* Russell, anyway?" Nana asked.

"He's okay. Learning to swim a little better."

"Are you teaching him?"

"I tried, but he wouldn't listen to me. Mom's been taking him for lessons."

Nana laughed a little breathlessly. "Russell, taking lessons—for anything!" she said. "He just doesn't seem like the type."

"Well, he'd *better* be the type for lessons," Cady said. "After all, he's about to start kindergarten."

"He is?" Nana asked, sounding amazed. "But he's still a baby, practically."

"Kids grow up fast," Cady said solemnly.

Nana laughed at her. "You sound like someone on a talk show," she teased. "The Tragedy of Today's Kids Growing Up Too Fast," she intoned, announcer-style. "Like we have a choice," she added in her normal voice.

"Well, you lose track of time more," Cady pointed out, "because you don't have any brothers or sisters."

"Thank goodness," Nana said. She had always liked being an only child. "I just wish—" She hesitated.

"What?" Cady asked, pouncing on the words. "What do you wish?"

Nana lowered her voice, though no one else was in the room. "I wish now that my mom and dad had another kid, and not only me. That's all."

"But, Nana—"

"And don't go telling me they have each other," Nana interrupted, bitter, "because you know it's not true. Not lately."

Cady thought about it; Nana was right, probably. The Webers *didn't* have each other anymore. Mr. Weber had his work, and he had Nana.

Mrs. Weber just had Nana.

"Do you think they're going to get a divorce?" Nana asked Cady, trying to sound casual about the question.

"I don't know," Cady said. "I think they're so busy with you being sick, and all—"

"I meant after I'm *gone,* Cady."

Gone. The word seemed to ring like a cold iron bell

in Cady's head. She inspected her knees, unable to look at Nana. "Um, would it really bother you if they got a divorce—then?" she finally asked her friend.

Nana twitched a shrug, looked down, and pleated the edge of her sheet. "I guess I'd rather they didn't," she said finally. "I don't know why. Maybe I don't want them to blame me when it finally happens."

"They wouldn't blame you," Cady said faintly.

"They might," Nana replied. "Oh, I know they weren't really happy before," she continued, "but it seemed like they could have gone on forever and ever that way—just a little bit miserable—until I got sick again, that is. When something this big went wrong, they couldn't pretend anymore."

"But it's nobody's fault you got sick," Cady objected.

"Oh, I don't mean they blame each other," Nana said, "but I think they're a *lot* miserable now. They kind of remind me of your bathing suit," Nana added, trying to make a joke of what she was saying. "You know, they've stretched about as much as they can stretch."

"Well, I don't think having another kid would make things any easier on them now," Cady said, pulling at a loose thread. "One kid can't replace another one. And I don't think another kid would keep them together, either—not if they're really going to split. Which I guess they probably are."

Nana looked at her, brown eyes narrowed. Finally she said, "Oh, Cady, you're just trying to cheer me up."

The two girls looked at one another for a second, then they burst out laughing.

The real Nana was back—for now, anyway.

• • •

"Everyone into the car," Cady's father said that evening. "We're off for some family fun. The traditional dinner and a movie!" His short hair was still wet from the after-work shower he had taken.

"Seat belt, Russell," Mrs. Winton said.

"Well, I'm not eating salad, and nobody can make me," Russell said. "Unless it's regular lettuce," he added. The last time they'd eaten in Pasadena's Old Town, Russell had been served a salad of field greens. He hadn't liked it, and that was putting things mildly.

"I have to admit I'm with Russell on the subject of salads," Cady said from the backseat. "I mean, I like different kinds of lettuce and everything, but some salads taste plain old nasty—like a person went into a vacant lot and hacked off a bunch of weeds. In my opinion. Oh," she added, "that reminds me—can we drive past the vacant lot at the top of the hill?" Cady hadn't seen the lot in a couple of weeks; she'd been avoiding it.

"Sure, no problem," her father said. Pine Crest made a loop around the top of the hill, so a car could drive in either direction and still end up at the bottom.

"Why do you want to see the vacant lot, honey?" her mother asked.

"I don't know. Just keeping track of the neighborhood, I guess."

"She and Nana are all mad that someone's going to build a house on it," Russell reported.

"Be quiet, Russell," Cady said. "Mind your own business."

"Well, here it is, for better or worse," Cady's father said, slowing the car down to a crawl. "Hey, they're working fast! But it doesn't look like the house will be *too* bad."

"Although it's hard to tell," her mother said. "They only have the foundation down and some of the framing completed. It's going to be big."

The Wintons gazed at the structure. The sun was going down behind it, and for a moment everything seemed to be outlined in light. Bushes that had been crushed by the construction workers, piles of lumber, even the insects that circled crazily in the twilight—everything seemed to glow all at once. It almost looked beautiful.

"I hope they have a pool. Or a dog, at least," Russell said gloomily.

"It'll be a while before we find out, Russ," his father said.

Just then, a fancy green car rounded the corner behind the Wintons, skidded to a halt inches from their rear bumper, and beeped impatiently three times. Cady was pretty sure she recognized the car; it was the same one that had slowed down to look at the lot when she'd been up there with Nana. Mr. Winton waved an apology and headed down the hill.

Nana's mom was right, Cady thought. It *was* dangerous around here.

• • •

Old Town was crowded, even though it was a Tuesday night. But it was a beautiful, mild evening, and it had been a hot, smoggy day. Lots of people felt like getting out.

I just hope I don't see anyone I know, Cady thought as they parked their car and walked to the restaurant. None of her friends was dating yet, but still, being out with your family was sort of like saying you didn't have anything better to do.

Not that there was anything especially wrong with her family, Cady thought—although she wished her parents wouldn't hold hands like that! And Russell was singing to himself again. That was kind of weird.

But—Cady had to admit it to herself—it felt kind of good to get away from Pine Crest Road, even if it was only for a little while.

She looked at the people strolling the crowded sidewalks, and her heart beat as fast as if she were Rip Van Winkle, just waking up.

At least it wasn't the weekend, Cady thought. That would be really lame, being in Old Town with your family then.

And at least school hadn't started yet. Cady felt as though she were floating in an in-between, end-of-summer time: last year's classmates were still lost in their own summer worlds, and next year remained a nerve-racking mystery. No, she thought, if she had to be out with her family, now was—

"Cady!" a voice called out, excited. Mr. Winton paused on the crowded sidewalk, hearing his daughter's name spoken. Everyone behind him had to stop, too, like cars piling up on the freeway. Someone grabbed Cady's arm. "Cady," the voice repeated. "Hi!"

"Oh, hi, Althea," Cady said, amazed that she'd remembered the girl's name. Althea went to Arroyo, too, and was even in her grade, and the grade wasn't all that big, but still, with everything that had been happening...

Everyone but Nana seemed unreal lately, somehow, Cady realized.

Althea's round, freckled face instantly turned serious, important, and she whispered, "I heard about poor Nana, how much she's changed. It's so sad, isn't it?"

"Cady, come on," Russell said, tugging at his sister's hand. "We're *starving*."

"Just a minute," Cady told him. She turned to Althea and said, "Nana's doing okay, really. She's barely changed at all."

Althea looked confused for a moment, and doubtful. "But she's not going to be coming back to Arroyo, is she?"

"Um, probably not," Cady admitted. "Not just at first."

Oh, come *on,* she told herself. Not *ever*. She didn't want to say that to Althea, though.

"Well," Althea said, her pale eyes wide with sincerity, "I think it's really wonderful what you're doing, Cady. Visiting her every day and everything. It must be terrible for you." People surged past Althea and the Wintons as though they were rocks in the middle of a stream.

"But how do you know—"

"My mom called Mrs. Weber to see if there was anything she could *do,*" Althea explained, lowering her voice again. "Mrs. Weber said no, and then she said how great you and your family were being about everything."

A vivid picture jumped into Cady's head: she could swing her arm back, open her hand wide, and *swing*.

She could slap Althea so hard that her stupid teeth would rattle!

"I'm not doing anything special, not really," Cady said in her calmest voice.

"Yes you are," Althea said firmly, shaking her head in amazement. "And you sound so together," she added. "I'm impressed!"

Then my work here on earth is done, Cady thought sarcastically, anger making her almost dizzy.

Who cared if Althea was impressed? Not Cady.

But who cared if Althea—and everyone, Cady guessed now—was talking about how sick Nana really was? Or how bad she looked?

Who cared?

Nana would care, Cady thought angrily. And *she* cared.

"Cady," Russell urged, "come on!" He clutched at his stomach.

"Althea, dear?" Cady's mother asked brightly. "Would you like to join us for dinner?"

No, no, *no!* Cady thought.

"Oh, no thanks, Mrs. Winton," Althea said, as if finally picking up a few of Cady's brain waves. "I'm supposed to be meeting up with my parents. But thanks anyway," she added.

Then she waved goodbye and disappeared into the crowd—which was now less than glittering, at least in Cady's eyes.

Chapter Six

Private Property

━━━━━━━

"HEY, RUSS, WANT TO GO for a walk?" It was Saturday morning, the last weekend before school started. Cady was babysitting Russell for her parents, who had gone grocery shopping.

Russell looked up from the pile of Legos that surrounded him. "A walk where?" he asked, suspicious.

"Oh, I thought up the hill," Cady said, trying to make it sound like fun.

"What's up there?"

"Lots of stuff, Russell," Cady said. She really only wanted to see Nana's vacant lot again—or rather, the new construction site. She wanted to pick some flowers and things to make a bouquet for Nana.

"There's nothing good up there," Russell objected.

"But maybe we'll see a dog," Cady said. Poor allergic Russell. "Moxie Lewis might be out," she added enticingly. Moxie was one of Russell's favorites.

"Okay," Russell said, brightening. He stood up, shedding Legos. "I can finish this later."

• • •

Cady and Russell trudged up Pine Crest Road. It was another hot day; Cady groaned inwardly as she thought about sitting in class next week. Why did school have to start during the hottest time of the year? At least being in seventh grade was going to be pretty cool. If only...

Cady held Russell's sticky hand as they walked past Nana's house, then past the Morgans' house. She squinted her eyes against the heat rising from the road's tarry surface. And it was only nine-thirty! During these hottest days of the year people tried to do their chores very early in the morning, then they came out again late in the afternoon. They stayed inside during the middle of the day if they could.

Eucalyptus trees swayed and clattered above Cady and Russell. The trees' long pointed leaves seemed almost to zing in the heat. Somewhere nearby a cranky squirrel made scolding noises, and a mockingbird answered him. "How far are we going, anyway?" Russell asked, panting slightly.

"Not much farther," Cady reassured him. "Just up there," she added, pointing with her free hand.

"Where that car honked at Daddy?" Russell asked.

"Yeah. You remember the weirdest things," Cady said.

"Well, how come—"

"I just want to pick some flowers and stuff for Nana, if it's okay with *you*."

But Cady's attempt at sarcasm was lost on Russell. "It's okay with me," he said, "but why don't you just pick her some from our garden?"

Because these would be more special to her, Cady thought fiercely. These would be from her own private lot. Or what should have been her lot someday.

"And where's Moxie Lewis?" Russell continued, looking around. "I thought you promised that he—"

"Look, he's probably taking a nap, okay?" Cady said. She hadn't promised anything! "Maybe he'll come running when he hears us," she added.

"Or smells us," Russell said, wiping a hand on his T-shirt before putting it back in Cady's hand. "We're here," he added, sounding disappointed.

Cady looked around. Her chest ached a little from the smog.

First, she looked past the sketchy structure of the house. Cady tried to remember how pretty the view was from here. She couldn't see the ocean today; she could barely see downtown L.A. The city's towers loomed gray through the smog. Russell squatted next to her in the dirt, picking up little rocks. "I could use these," he said, "for my turtles." He cradled the rocks in his T-shirt with one hand.

Next, Cady looked at the house itself, or what would be the house when it was finished. No, she thought, she couldn't tell anything about it yet; it looked about the same as it had when they'd driven by last Tuesday.

Big.

Maybe the house wouldn't be too bad when it was done, she thought. You could still look *around* it and see the view. Maybe—

"Aren't you going to get some flowers? For Nana?" Russell reminded her. He scratched his dusty ankle.

"Oh, yeah, I guess," Cady said. She looked around once more. What could she pick? Everything looked dead, she thought.

Of course, that wasn't the new owner's fault, she reminded herself. Anything would dry to a crisp in this baking weather if it wasn't being watered. And why should someone waste precious water on a lot full of weeds?

Still, Cady thought grouchily, she didn't see why the construction workers had to run over all these bushes. She snapped a piece of mustard plant from a broken branch and then started searching for other things to add to Nana's bouquet.

Russell hummed, a distant siren sounded, a jay squawked, a dog barked, and underneath these sounds a lawn mower droned somewhere down the hill.

Later, Cady thought it was strange that she hadn't heard the car pull up. But maybe the heat and the mingled summer sounds had made her drowsy.

"Hey! Hey, you kids!" a voice bellowed.

Cady and Russell looked up quickly, stunned by the angry blast. "Hey," the man repeated, opening his car door. It was a dark green Jaguar, some part of Cady's mind noted. The same car that—

"That's the car that honked at Daddy," Russell whispered.

"Don't you kids know this is private property?" the man was shouting. "What do I have to do, fence off the whole site? Jeez." His face was red with rage.

Russell stood up, rocks forgotten, and groped for Cady's hand as the man strode toward them. Cady gripped her little brother's now-clammy hand and took a step back.

"This isn't a playground, you know," the man said, coming to a halt. He stood before them, almost blocking the sun, hands on his hips. Cady could smell his cologne.

She cleared her throat and tried to speak. "We were just—"

"Trespassing," the man said, finishing her sentence in triumph. "Now get out," he added. "And I don't want to see you kids back here, got that? *Ever.*"

"Come on, Russell," Cady mumbled. She tugged at her brother slightly. He seemed to be rooted where he stood.

"And you can just leave *those,* young lady," the man said, looking at the bunch of weeds Cady still held clenched in her hand.

Russell finally spoke. "But—but why? You don't need them," he objected, his voice shrill. "And anyway, they're for—"

"Shhh," Cady hissed at him. She didn't want Russell saying Nana's name out loud—not to this horrible man. She dropped the weeds and brushed her hands off on her shorts.

"Now beat it," the man said. "And don't come back, hear?"

• • •

"But that's terrible," Nana said later that day. Outrage had brought color to her cheeks, and her brown eyes glinted with some of their old energy. "He's brand-new, and we've lived in this neighborhood forever. Just who does he think he is, anyway?"

"He thinks he's the guy who owns that property, that's who," Cady said, glum—but pleased at Nana's reaction. "And I didn't even tell you everything."

"There's *more?*"

"Russell started crying on the way home," Cady reported. Russell hardly ever cried. "You should have seen my mom," she added. "She was ready to run up the hill and tear the guy apart."

Nana smiled a little; Mrs. Winton was tiny but tough. "What did your dad say?"

"Nothing much," Cady said, "but I could tell he was

really mad. You can see his jaw muscles sort of jump around when that happens, and his voice gets higher."

Nana yawned, patting at her mouth a second after the yawn stopped. Little things like this were happening more and more, Cady had noticed; it was as though Nana was out of focus somehow. Nana frowned, and reached for her pain clicker.

"Are you hurting?" Cady asked, leaning forward anxiously.

She had often heard Irene ask, *On a scale of one to ten, Nana, how bad is your pain?* Cady wanted to ask Nana that question now, but she didn't know what she would do with the answer.

"It's not too bad," Nana said after a moment.

Not too bad! But what did that mean? How bad *was* Nana's pain, Cady wondered—and where did it hurt?

Cady remembered that when she had been in nursery school, another kid had bumped into her while she was drinking from the water fountain, and she'd cut her lip. She'd run crying into the playground, bleeding. A teacher had finally caught up to her and—seeing the blood—had asked, "Where does it hurt?"

"Over there, at the drinking fountain," Cady had cried.

Suddenly now, watching Nana, Cady could remember how she'd felt when she was little, and she thought: if she could only get Nana out of bed, out of this house where all the pain was, maybe everything would be okay. Maybe—

"Cady?" Nana was saying.

"Mmm?"

"I think I want to take a nap now. Is that okay?"

"Sure," Cady said. "I'll come back later if you want."

"Yeah, okay," Nana said, already half asleep.

Irene was fixing herself a cup of tea in the Webers' kitchen. Cady said goodbye to her and shut the heavy front door as quietly as she could.

Even the birds were quiet now, in the afternoon heat. The only sound Cady could hear was of cars going by, way off down the hill.

She lowered her eyelids against the sun's glare as she walked home. She looked down at the road through her lashes; they seemed to sparkle with rainbow colors.

Cady's dad was pulling into the driveway as she got home. All his car windows were up, and air conditioning ruffled his hair as he beat time on the steering wheel with an open hand. Cady could hear the thrum of his music. He saw her, turned off the engine, and opened the car door. "Cady," he said. "Just the person I wanted to see."

"Hi, Dad," she said, looking in the car's backseat for grocery sacks. He put the front seat forward, retrieved a towel, and draped it over the steering wheel in an attempt to keep it cool.

"Uh, what did you want me to carry?"

"What? Oh, nothing. I just meant I was happy to *see* you. Gee, talk about suspicious. No," he continued as they shut the front door behind them, grateful to be inside the cool house, "it's just that you're starting school on Monday."

"I know, Dad," Cady said patiently.

"And once *that* happens, who knows when your mother and I will see you again?" he said, attempting a joke. "Want some lemonade?"

"Sure," Cady said suspiciously. She waited while he poured them each a glassful. She knew he wasn't finished yet.

"Ahhh," Mr. Winton said after gulping down half his drink.

"Um, so, Dad? What did you want to talk about, really?" Cady traced around a big square tile with one brown, sandaled foot.

"Am I that transparent?" he asked, making a funny face. He finished his lemonade in another gulp, then put the empty glass in the sink.

"Better put that in the dishwasher or Mom's going to yell," Cady advised, reminding him of the family rule.

"Oh, right," her dad said hastily, and he sloshed some water in the glass and jammed it into a crowded rack. "Let's sit down for a minute." He pulled out a kitchen chair for Cady.

She sat down, thinking hard. What had she done? Was he going to get all mad at her about going up to the vacant lot that morning?

Or was this about Nana again?

"I've been thinking, Cady," her father said. "I'm really very glad school is starting on Monday."

"You are?" Cady asked, straightening a place mat. "How come?"

"Your mother and I—well, it's no secret that we've been worried about you, honey."

"I told you, you guys don't have to worry about me, Dad."

"We can't help it, Cady. I guess worrying is what parents do best. But we feel it's important for you to start the new school year with—well, with an open mind, Cady. With a good attitude."

"I don't know what you're talking about," Cady said, confused—and a little bit huffy. "My attitude's okay."

"I'm talking about making new friends, baby. Give it a

chance, at least. Your mother and I don't want you rushing home from school every single day to go sit with Nana for hours and hours. I mean, visiting her is fine, Cady. But we also want you to make room for other things, other people. Life has to go on."

Cady jumped up, skidding her chair back along the bumpy red tiles. "I can't believe you're saying this, Dad," she said. "I've been doing stuff with the family, haven't I? And taking care of Russell sometimes?"

"Well, yes," her father said. "But—"

"I can't believe you're actually *saying* this," Cady repeated. She pounded her fist on the table. Then she stood there, trembling.

"Cady, sit down," her father said in his most soothing voice, the one he probably used with people whose houses needed retrofitting to make them safer in earthquakes. "Listen to me, baby. I'm not saying you should turn your back on Nana. Just cool it a little, maybe. And it's not only me who thinks so, it's your mother, too."

"Don't—call—me—*baby*," Cady said, pausing between each word. "I'm not your baby anymore!"

"I know you're not," her father said, "but you're not talking to us, either. Cady, you have to talk about what's happening to Nana. And what's happening to you, too. If you can't talk to your mother or me, maybe you could talk to someone else. A psychologist, maybe?"

"No!" Cady shouted. She wanted to keep Nana to herself, she thought angrily.

"Well, I want you to think about it, anyway," her father said firmly.

"God, can't anything be private around here?" Cady cried. "You guys just want me to turn my back on Nana and move on to the next thing, don't you? Just so you can stop worrying about me!"

"Cady, that's not fair. Your mother and I *love* Nana. And Mommy is doing everything she can to help Mrs. Weber, you know that. Groceries, chores, and hand-holding. They've been friends for a long time, remember. It's just that we—"

Cady lowered her voice. She could barely control it, she was so angry. "You really want this to be over with, don't you?" She shook her head slowly. "You guys just don't get it."

"Get what, Cady?" her father asked. "All we want is for you to talk to us!"

"You just don't get it," Cady repeated dully. "You want it *all* to be over, which means Nana will be dead, by the way, in case you hadn't figured that out."

"Cady, you're not being—"

"She'll be *dead* then," Cady insisted. "And what *I* want..." She hesitated.

"What do you want, Cady?" her father asked softly.

"I want it to go on forever, Dad," she said.

I'm sorry, Nana, she added to herself, *but I don't want to lose you.*

And Cady guessed that was one more thing to feel guilty about.

Chapter Seven

A Secret

▬▬▬

THE ARROYO SCHOOL, called the Arroyo Seco Institute for Young Ladies at the turn of the century, was still a girls' school in spite of the name change. Opening assembly had just let out, and the broad tiled hallway echoed with the sound of middle- and upper-school girls lining up in front of small tables for their class schedules.

Cady went to the far corner of the hall where the T–Z table was. *Winton* and *Weber.* She remembered the start of sixth grade last year, when she and Nana had peeked in the door and watched the older girls get in line. The two of them had been so excited—next year *they* would do that! They would finally get to have a different teacher for each course.

Now Cady was back at Arroyo again, but all alone—or as alone as you could be in a roomful of squawking people.

"Cady?" someone behind her said.

Cady turned. "Oh, hi, Ellen," she said. Ellen Webster had been in her sixth-grade class last year. With Nana.

"Hi," Ellen said. "Did you have a good summer? You look great."

"Thanks," Cady said. "You too." She gazed around the noisy room.

"I had a much better tan, but it faded," Ellen said, holding out an arm, as if for inspection.

She thought *she* had problems, Cady thought, disgusted. Wasn't she even going to ask about—

"So how's Nana doing?" Ellen said, lowering her voice. Now she wore her most serious expression, the one people seemed to paste on their faces nowadays when they said the word *Nana*. "Not too good, I hear," Ellen added, shaking her head solemnly.

"Oh, I don't know," Cady said, disagreeing instantly—and automatically. She flipped her hair back over her shoulder. Every time she'd been forced to talk about Nana lately, she thought, she'd regretted it. Her words seemed to make Nana's illness ordinary, somehow, when it wasn't ordinary at all, it was terrible. And wrong!

Wrong. That was the most important thing, Cady thought, but no one seemed to understand. Not that it was any of their business.

"Althea told me all the stuff you're doing for Nana," Ellen was saying. "Everyone thinks it's just wonderful, Cady." Now Ellen's face wore a sickening-sweet expression that Cady hated—it seemed so phony.

"Well, thanks," Cady mumbled, not knowing what else to say. She felt dizzy with anger, though. At Ellen, at Althea, and at herself.

She was kind of miffed at Nana, too, she realized, startled. *Really* miffed.

"Cady Winton?" a woman's voice said. "You're next, dear."

• • •

The day continued in what felt like slow motion to Cady. She waited in line for her books; she went to first period.

She was going to die of old age before the first day of school was over, she thought. That would be a laugh—for Nana, anyway. Well, maybe it would be better than getting hit by that killer bus they used to talk about.

But Cady sat in each shortened first-day class, pretending to pay attention. She took notes. She *participated*— well, you had to at Arroyo. They prided themselves on that; the classes were so small.

Finally, it was time for lunch.

Cady had been dreading lunch all morning. She kept hearing her lame response to Ellen that morning: *Well, thanks!* She pictured Nana's classmates surrounding her in the shade of the lunch patio's Chinese elms. She worried over the questions they would ask. . . .

Was Nana ever coming back?

Was she really dying?

How did she look?

"Oh, I'm afraid her tan's kind of lousy," Cady imagined herself answering them, "but she's nice and thin now." They would all be intrigued by *that* news.

No, anything she would say to them about Nana would end up feeling as though it were a betrayal—of her best friend, and of their friendship.

• • •

"Um, are you already sitting with someone at lunch, or can I sit with you?" a girl was asking Cady, who was hiding by her locker. "I don't know how it works here."

It was the new kid from Cady's history class. She'd been introduced to everyone, but Cady couldn't remember her name. "Well, sure, I guess you can sit with me," Cady said, feeling awkward.

"I'm Laura," the girl said. Her dark brown hair hung in a thick braid down her back, and her blue eyes sparkled as if she knew Cady had forgotten her name. "You're Cady, aren't you?"

"Mmm-hmm," Cady agreed, nodding *yes.* "Want to go over there by the fountain? It looks cooler."

And it was far, far away from the usual lunchtime group sitting under the elms.

"Okay," Laura said.

They settled down on the shade-dappled tiled ledge that surrounded the fountain, chasing off two small birds who had been getting a drink. "Bird-watchers call those LBJs," Laura said, nodding in the birds' direction.

"They do?" Cady asked through a mouthful of peach yogurt.

"Yeah—it stands for Little Brown Jobs," Laura said. "Pretty technical, huh?"

Cady grinned. "Are you a bird-watcher?"

"Not me," Laura said, shaking her head. "My mom is, though. Sandra MacLean, attorney at law. But she's also a birder in her spare time, such as it is."

"Huh," Cady said. She tried to imagine a bird-watching lawyer. *Objection, Your Honor,* the woman might cry, springing to her feet in the courtroom. *That was a mockingbird, not a scrub jay!* "Sandra MacLean, attorney at law," Cady repeated. "That sounds like a TV series."

"Probably will be, someday," Laura agreed. "My dad's name is Howard McAllister."

"Attorney at law?" Cady asked.

"No, he's a sculptor," Laura said, laughing.

"Cool," Cady said, impressed.

"My parents aren't divorced or anything," Laura told

her, "they just kept their own last names—and gave them both to me. Laura MacLean McAllister. Two Macs. We just moved here last summer, from Oakland."

"Cool," Cady repeated.

She liked sitting here with Laura, talking about nothing, she realized. It was hot. The spray bouncing from the upturned concrete shell in the fountain evaporated before it could even land on them. Cady reached her hand out to try to touch it.

"What about you?" Laura asked after taking a drink from her thermos.

"Me? Oh, I've lived here forever," Cady said. "I live on the other side of the arroyo, up Pine Crest, with my parents and my little brother."

She didn't mention Nana. Laura would hear all about her soon enough, Cady thought.

Besides, it was so great talking with someone who didn't even *know* Nana!

• • •

But the bad part about meeting Laura—and liking Laura, Cady thought as the afternoon wore on—was that now she had a secret. For just about the first time, there was something she couldn't tell Nana.

After all, as Cady confessed only to herself, the old, friendly Nana seemed gradually to have turned into kind of a grouch. When Cady told her about going to a new movie, for instance, Nana had said, "Gee, rub my nose in it, why don't you?" And when Cady had brought her new school supplies over for Nana to inspect, her friend had turned her head away without saying a word.

So how would Nana feel about something as important as a brand-new friend?

We never used to have secrets, Cady thought, chewing her lower lip. But this was one she would have to keep.

After all, Nana needed her more than ever now—and she couldn't be upset.

It was actually kind of cool being needed so much, Cady admitted to herself.

Still, she found herself dawdling at her empty house after she got home from school. Russell was at day care following his first day of kindergarten, and her parents were still at work.

Cady changed out of her uniform, then she washed her hands, then she drank a big glass of lemonade, then she s-l-o-w-l-y went through the mail. She divided it up on the hall table: a magazine, bills, a postcard from Aunt Margaret in San Francisco.

She watered all the houseplants, then she washed her hands again.

Cady chewed at a ragged thumbnail as she stared out the window. It was so smoggy that she couldn't even see the San Gabriels. Did she really have to go see Nana today? She could say she'd had to stay late at school or something....

No, she thought finally—that would be lying. And it would only make things worse if she put off going over there. She might as well get it over with.

• • •

An extra car was in the Webers' driveway. The sound of giggles floated down the hall leading to Nana's bedroom as Cady let herself in the front door. She hesitated, startled at the sound. Then she called out, "Hello?"

Irene poked her curly head out of Nana's room and beckoned. "Hi, Cady! Come on in—there's someone I want you to meet."

Cady entered Nana's room, wishing she'd stayed home. If she'd known there was going to be this crowd . . .

The head of Nana's bed was cranked upright, and a tray straddled her legs. On the tray was a muffin tin with colored beads in it. At Nana's bedside, a nurse Cady had never seen before fiddled with the pain medicine box while Mrs. Weber watched, looking more relaxed than she had in a while. "Hey, Cady," Nana said cheerfully. "Wait until you see what Irene and I have been doing!"

"I think you should introduce Cady to Heather, darling," Mrs. Weber said, like they were all at a tea party or something, Cady thought.

"Oh, yeah—sorry," Nana said. "This is Heather, Cady. She's the head nurse, the RN from hospice. I told you about her—she comes once a week."

Heather looked up from what she was doing and smiled. Her graying hair was pulled up high and tight into a ponytail, and the stethoscope hanging at her neck was slung back over one plump, round shoulder. Heather's white doctor-style coat was open over jeans and a T-shirt. There was a beeper at her waist. "Glad to meet you, Cady," Heather said. "Nana's told me all about you. I'm surprised we haven't bumped into each other before now."

"Well, I'm here a lot," Cady said, feeling as though she needed to show that she was even *more* surprised. "Nearly every day," she added.

"I've heard," Heather said with a friendly nod. Her ponytail bounced. She bent back to her task, softly explaining something to Mrs. Weber, who then jotted a few words in a notebook.

"Irene and I have been beading," Nana said, holding up a partly finished strand. "She's an expert."

"Oh, no, not really," Irene objected, laughing. "But there's this bead store near my apartment—"

"And so she brought over some beads," Nana said, happily finishing Irene's sentence. "These are from Mexico," she added, holding up a small silvery object.

"They're pretty," Cady said, feeling awkward. "*I* could have brought you beads," she added. "There's this brand-new place near the supermarket, over by school."

"Really?" Nana said, fingering the necklace she was making. "You never said."

"Well, I didn't know you were interested."

Heather stood up and stretched. "That ought to do it," she said, grinning at Nana. "You feeling better now?"

"Yeah, thanks," Nana said, shifting a little uncomfortably in her bed. "But I think, I think—"

"You'd like some privacy for a few minutes, right?" Heather said. *Privacy* was the code word for when Nana needed to use the bedpan, Cady had learned. "Cady," Heather continued, "why don't you and I go into the living room? Then I'll talk with Nana's mother again, before I leave."

"There are drinks in the fridge," Mrs. Weber said. "Help yourselves."

• • •

Cady followed Heather down the hall and plunked herself down on the Webers' sofa. She looked around.

Stacks of old newspapers and magazines were piled on the coffee table. Heather picked up three dirty coffee mugs and walked into the kitchen with them. "Want a soda or something?" she called over her shoulder.

"No thanks," Cady called back. She was thirsty, but she didn't want Heather bringing her things. In fact, she didn't want anything to do with Hospice Heather.

It felt weird being in the living room again, Cady thought, sitting on this sofa—without Nana. She and Nana had spent so many hours in this room, so many *years*. . . .

It looked completely different now. Throw pillows were squashed deep into the corners of chairs, dust dulled every surface, wilted flower arrangements sat dying on the mantel. Cady wrinkled her nose; she could even smell stinky old flower water!

Disgusted, she turned to look out the sliding glass doors that led to the Webers' deck. Past the fingerprint-smudged glass she saw the big clay pots in which Mrs. Weber usually took such pride. Full of the dried, bent relics of flowers, they now looked pathetic. A row of tiny birds sat on the deck's redwood railing, swooping down in relays to scrabble in the pots' hardened dirt.

LBJs, Cady thought, remembering Laura's words with satisfaction. *Little Brown Jobs.*

But she wasn't going to tell Nana that.

Hey, Cady thought, scowling suddenly, if Nana can have such a good time stringing beads without me all afternoon, then I can have fun without her, too.

Chapter Eight

Forever

"CADY, I THINK WE should talk," Heather said, coming back into the Webers' living room with a glass of water.

Cady stood up and tugged her T-shirt where it clung to her back. "I—I can't stay, really. I have to be getting home pretty soon."

"Can't you stick around just a little while?" the nurse asked, raising her dark eyebrows comically. "I'm not going to bite." Cady sat down again. "I thought maybe you might have some questions about Nana, about what's happening to her." Heather chewed on an ice cube for a second. "About what's going to happen," she corrected herself.

"Well—no, I guess not," Cady said, pretending to give Heather's comment some thought. "I mean, she seems really good lately. Doesn't she?"

Heather tilted her head, but she didn't argue— or agree.

"Then that's all that matters," Cady concluded. She shrugged unconvincingly.

"That's certainly the most important thing," Heather said, "but I wouldn't say it's all that matters, Cady. Part of hospice—part of my job—is to look out for the folks *around* the person who is dying. Did you know that?"

Why does she have to use the word *dying?* Cady thought, frowning. Does she think I don't know what's happening, or something?

Heather sighed. "It's hard, Cady, even for me, and I've gone through this a lot. But most people have never been around someone who is dying. They don't know what to expect, and it can make them scared."

Cady was indignant. "I'm not—what do you mean, they don't know what to expect?" she asked suddenly. "Do you mean they don't know what the dying is going to be like?"

Heather nodded.

"Well," Cady asked after a moment, "what *is* it going to be like?" She felt as if the words had been dragged out of her.

"For Nana, it will probably just quietly happen," Heather said, sitting down. "Not for a while, though. She'll go on getting weaker, and maybe she'll start needing her pain clicker more, but we'll take care of that."

"I can help," Cady said fiercely. She flexed her hand as if she were clicking the button at that very moment.

Heather nodded. "After that, it's pretty likely that Nana will slip into a coma, Cady. And then she'll die, while she's in the coma. That's what death will probably be like for Nana."

"Oh," Cady said. She felt one shoulder go up in a tiny shrug. She picked up a dusty throw pillow and clasped it to her chest. She looked down, waiting for it to rise and fall with one of her breaths.

"For us it will be harder, in a way," Heather continued. "We may have to watch Nana get a little confused and irritable. She might have trouble talking or even listening. Then she'll get weaker. She'll sleep more, and then it won't really be sleep, it will be the coma. That might go on for quite a while. Then her breathing might start to sound ragged, and her breaths might come farther and farther apart."

"That sounds terrible," Cady whispered.

"It will just be everything in her body slowing down, getting ready for the end," Heather said, "but it's not likely to be terrible for Nana."

"Well, does *she* know what it will be like?" Cady asked.

The nurse nodded. "She asked, and I told her," she said.

"What does she say about it?" Cady wanted to know—she *had* to know.

"She says she's worried for you guys. For her mom, especially, and for you," Heather reported.

"For *me*? She's the one who's dying, and she's worried about me?" Cady couldn't believe her ears.

"You're her best friend, Cady. Of course she worries about you!" Heather said, surprised. "She knows you're having a big problem with this."

"Well, who wouldn't?" Cady said, feeling that she had to defend herself. "I just didn't think she could tell. I've been trying to hide it."

"Oh, Nana can tell, all right," Heather said, smiling. "She said she told you once how angry she was this was happening to her, and you didn't really want to talk about it. You tried to change the subject, she said."

"I—I don't remember that," Cady said, but she did, a little.

"Well, don't you dare feel bad about it, if you ever do remember it," Heather said. "You're doing a terrific job, Cady."

"Being a friend isn't a job," Cady objected.

"Oh, sure it is—sometimes, at least, honey. I *know* it is,

in fact," Heather said, fiddling with her stethoscope. "Look at today, for instance," she continued. "Here you are, on your first day of school and everything, and I'll bet no one's even asked you how it went."

"But how did *you* know it was my first day of school?" Cady asked. "Even Nana doesn't have the slightest idea anymore."

"Sure she does," Heather said. "She's been blue about it for days, Cady. Irene told me that's why she brought in all those beads, so Nana could do something special today, too."

"But—but she never said anything to *me* about being sad," Cady said, feeling ashamed—and a little angry. "And I thought she was telling me everything."

"Do you still tell her everything?" Heather asked, as if she already knew the answer.

Cady blushed, and she bit her lower lip.

"Don't feel bad," Heather consoled her. "Little things about a friendship change all the time, Cady, even when everything's perfectly normal. Nothing ever stays the same." She stood up and stretched. "But it's pretty obvious to all of us that you two still have what you always had," she added, smiling. "Best friends—that's never going to change. It'll last forever."

"Sort of, anyway," Cady said bitterly, thinking of those last ragged breaths Heather had described.

"No," Heather said firmly, "it'll last forever. You'll see."

• • •

Cady walked slowly down Pine Crest later that afternoon. In spite of what Heather had said about Cady's friendship with Nana lasting forever, Cady couldn't help but think about how it had *already* changed. It wasn't simply that she no longer told

Nana everything, Cady admitted to herself, but Nana herself was different. She was so self-absorbed these days, and cranky, and...and boring. If I met her now for the first time, would I even *want* to be her friend? Cady asked herself.

She stopped walking for a moment; she didn't know the answer.

The sharp smell of charcoal lighter fluid hung in the air, a sure sign that someone was trying to cook dinner outside. Cady's head ached with fatigue; she felt so tired that her first day as a seventh grader seemed to have happened at least a week earlier, not that very day.

And naturally there was homework already, she thought, disgusted, as she resumed her walk. Eager to show how tough they were going to be, Arroyo teachers never missed the opportunity to hand out assignments the first day of school. But all Cady really wanted to do was to eat a bowl of cereal and climb into bed.

• • •

Everyone had arrived home. The Wintons' two cars were parked side by side in the driveway. Their garage was so stuffed full of old wading pools, croquet sets, and stacks of newspaper for school paper drives that there was no hope of squeezing a car inside.

Cady opened the front door as quietly as she could.

"Hi, Cady!" Russell said, pouncing on her. He was wearing a pair of sweatpants and a tattered nylon cape.

Cady hoped he hadn't gone to school dressed that way. "Hey, Russ," she said. "How was your first day of kindergarten?"

Russell's face took on a strange expression. "It was okay," he mumbled.

"He says he's not going back tomorrow," Cady's mother announced, coming into the hall with a laundry basket on her hip.

"How come? What happened?" Cady asked.

"Nothing *happened*," Russell said, sounding as if he had explained this a hundred times already. "I went. It was fun, just like you said."

"So why aren't you going back?" Cady asked him.

"I didn't say I'd never go back," Russell pointed out, straightening his cape as if he was about to pose for a picture. "Maybe next week I will," he said. He smiled, showing all his teeth.

"Russell, I hate to be the one to break this to you," Mrs. Winton said, "but you're going to have to go to school five days a week from now on."

"For the next thirteen years," Cady added.

"Nuh-*uh*," Russell said, serene as he shook his head *no*.

"Yuh-*huh*," Cady nodded her head *yes*.

"Nuh-*uh*. I never went before and it was okay. So how come everything has to change?"

"It just does," Cady said bleakly.

"Nuh-*uh*."

"Come on, you two—break it up," their mother said. "Russell, we'll talk about this some more after supper. But right now, your father has something delicious burning on the grill out back. Why don't we go keep him company?"

This was really more of an order than a suggestion, so off they went, almost without another word.

• • •

Russell spent even longer in the bath than usual, chattering with his toys. Cady could hear him through her bedroom wall. She couldn't make out the exact words, but it sounded as though there were lots of people in the tub with him. Russell was good at making up voices.

She peeked into her brother's room a little later. Her mother was standing by the bathroom door trying to coax Russell out. Mrs. Winton turned to Cady and shrugged helplessly, raising her palms to the ceiling.

"Oh, all *right*," Russell finally said from behind the door. He came out wrapped in a navy-blue towel that looked as though it went around him two or three times. His red hair glistened, standing up in tiny spikes.

"Let's lay out your clothes for tomorrow, sweetie," his mother said in a cheerful voice. "Isn't that a good idea, Cady?" she added, as if trying to get everyone involved. "That way, you'll be sure to look nice, Russ."

"I'm not wearing clothes tomorrow," Russell announced. "I already decided."

At least he'd stopped saying that he wasn't going to school, Cady noticed; that was progress.

"Russell, you can't go to school bare," his mother said, trying not to smile.

"Why not? Who cares? Lots of kids go bare," Russell said, sounding like an old pro.

"People would care," Cady said. "Trust me on this one, Russ."

"Oh, okay," Russell said, grudging. "I'll wear my cape."

• • •

"Russell says he can't get to sleep. He wants to talk with you," Mrs. Winton said an hour later, poking her head into Cady's room. She shrugged an apology to Cady, who groaned slightly as she looked up from her blue canvas

notebook. "What?" her mother asked. "Are you writing the
What I Did on My Summer Vacation essay?"

"I *wish*. No, nothing that interesting," Cady said,
getting up. "He's wearing his pajamas, I hope."

"I insisted, if he's going to have a visitor. Don't stay
too long, though. It's a school night—with any luck." Mrs.
Winton raised a hand, showing crossed fingers.

"Okay," Cady said. She padded down the hall in her
bare feet. Her brother's bedside light—in the shape of a big
red crayon—was still on, and she could hear Russell singing
under his breath.

*"This old man! He played twelve! He played knick-knack on
his melve!"* he warbled.

"Hey, Russ," Cady interrupted. His striped pajamas
were buttoned clear up to his chin.

"Oh, hi! I thought maybe you were at Nana's again,"
Russell said, scooting over to make room for her on his bed.

"No, I was just doing some homework," Cady said as
she settled back against an extra pillow.

Russell's expression turned gloomy. "Oh, homework. We didn't get any today." A stubborn look spread
over his face.

"In kindergarten? Russell, I don't think you *are* going
to get any. I wouldn't worry about that if I were you."

"Well, I'm not doing it, no matter what." He scowled,
and the skin along his cheekbones paled a little, making his
freckles stand out like dashes of cinnamon. "And they can't
make me," he added.

"Why are you getting all worked up over nothing?"
Cady asked.

"It's not *nothing*," Russell said, indignant. "Are you
going back there tonight?"

"Back where?"

"You know. To Nana's house."

"Oh," Cady said. "No, not tonight."

"*Good,*" her brother said fervently, and he sighed.

"Russell, is that what's really bothering you? That I'm over at Nana's a lot?" Cady asked.

"I just don't think you should go," he mumbled.

"Tonight?"

"*Ever.*"

Cady turned to look at her brother: he had slid down in bed until his head was jammed against the bottom of his scrunched-up pillow. "Russell," she said, amazed, "are you still jealous of Nana?"

"No, I'm *scared* of her!" he blurted out.

"But—why on earth?" Cady almost fell off the edge of the bed. "Russell," she said, "Nana's not contagious or anything. You can't catch what she has. You can't catch cancer."

"Yes you can," he said stubbornly.

"No, Russell, you definitely *can't*. You're wrong about this one."

"I can prove it," he insisted. "You're sad all the time, right? And it's all because of Nana. You caught *that* from her, didn't you? But nobody is supposed to talk about it, like there's nothing wrong, right?"

Cady was perplexed. Wrong? Right?

"Mom and Dad talk about it all the time," she said, her voice faint.

"No they don't, not so much. All they talk about is you, anymore. You, you, you, never me! And that's boring! They're sad, and it's all because of you and that stupid contagious Nana."

"Nana's not stupid, she's dying," Cady said angrily. There, she'd said it to him for the very first time—was he happy now? He'd *made* her say it.

"So don't go," he cried, suddenly clinging to her.

Cady was astounded. She squeezed him back; he sobbed. "Russell, *I'm* not going to die."

"You could," he hiccuped, wiping his nose against her T-shirt. "If Nana can die, so could you. Everything's changing!"

Cady didn't even yell at him about his runny nose. That shirt was going in the hamper anyway. "Russell—" she began.

"First Tommy," he interrupted. Tommy, one of Russell's turtles, had been found hunkered stonelike in the corner of the terrarium two weeks earlier. "And then Nana," Russell continued, "and next maybe you."

"Russell, I—"

"Mom says Tommy is gone forever," Russell interrupted with a noisy sniff. "Disappeared! We had to bury him. I wanted to wait," he added, remembering the fight he'd had with his mother.

Let's give him another chance, Russell had pleaded.

"No, you can't wait," Cady said dully.

"So now he's dead, and there's just Joe and Richard left, and they miss him. I can tell," he added fiercely, as though Cady were doubting him.

But she didn't doubt him. "I know they do," she said.

"Turtles have feelings too," Russell insisted.

"I agree. But Russell, that's just it. Don't you see?"

"What's just it?" Russell asked, stifling a yawn.

"They *miss* him. There has to be something still there for them to miss, or they wouldn't miss it in the first place, right?"

"I don't know what you're talking about," Russell said.

"See, Tommy isn't really gone forever," Cady said, excited. "Well, it's sort of forever, but part of him—the memory of him—is still here, Russ."

"He's in the dirt. *All* of him," Russell said drowsily. "Face it, Cady."

"Yeah, but Russell, don't you see—"

Russell snuggled down into the covers and said, "You better go now. I have school tomorrow, don't forget."

Chapter Nine

Friends

"I'M SORRY ABOUT YOUR FRIEND," Laura said after school one day. She reached up to yank at a drooping eucalyptus branch, and two or three nuts clattered to the sidewalk.

Cady sighed. "Thanks," she said. "Who told you?" Laura was waiting for her father to pick her up, and Cady was keeping her company before walking home.

Laura shrugged. "Everybody told me," she said, smiling a little. "What did you think would happen? You know school. What else is there to talk about?"

"Nothing," Cady said, laughing. "It's just that nobody ever says anything to *me* about it nowadays."

"They're scared to," Laura reported promptly. "Ever since you yelled at Althea that day in P.E."

"She was getting on my nerves," Cady said, blushing at the memory. After all, the only thing Althea had done was to ask *How is poor Nana?* once too often.

Now Laura was the one to sigh. "Well," she said, "what with you going bonkers, and Nana's mother telling kids on the phone that Nana had said she didn't want any visitors..." Her voice trailed away.

"I don't know why Nana decided that," Cady said. "The hospice nurse wasn't too surprised, though. I guess

Nana feels funny about the way she looks, and the least little thing gets her so tired that she can't see straight. And she feels sick to her stomach nearly all the time. I guess she just can't concentrate on anything else but being sick. Maybe that's it."

"It's good that she still wants to see *you,* though," Laura said, looking at Cady sideways.

"Yeah, I guess," Cady said, kicking at a leaf. "I can't believe you'll never get to meet her now," she added sadly. "You'll just hear what other people say about her."

"Do you think we would have been friends?" Laura asked, curious.

Cady thought about this for a moment. "Probably not," she finally admitted with a laugh. "Nana's kind of the possessive type when it comes to best friends. So I guess she'd be jealous of you."

Laura smiled, obviously pleased at Cady's words. Then she started waving her one free arm in the air. "There he is!" she said.

A yellow pickup truck swerved up to the curb, and a shaggy-haired man leaned over to unlock the passenger door. "Hi, babe!" he called out through the open window.

"Is that your *dad?*" Cady asked, impressed.

Laura laughed out loud. "What," she asked, "did you think he was just some guy? Of course it's my dad! Hi, Daddy," she said.

"Hey, is that the famous Cady Winton?" the man asked.

Cady stepped forward, shy. "Hi, Mr. McAllister," she said.

"This is perfect," the man said, grinning. "Look," he said to Laura, "I have to go into Old Town, to meet this guy for coffee for—oh, I don't know, maybe an hour. Talk about some work. Do you and Cady want to come, too?"

Laura turned to Cady. Her eyes were bright with excitement. "Can you?" she asked.

"I—I think so," Cady said, her heart beating fast. "But I'd have to call my mom and ask."

Laura's father fished in his pocket, then he held up a quarter. "Is there a pay phone near here?" he asked. He looked around, as if one might sprout on a nearby tree at any moment.

"Yes, next to the office," Cady said.

Laura grabbed the coin. "We'll be right back," she called out.

She and Cady tossed down their backpacks and ran to the phone. Cady stuffed the quarter into the slot and dialed.

"Hello?" Mrs. Winton said, picking up the receiver.

"Hi, Mom?" Cady said. "Laura's dad wants to know if I can go with them to Old Town for an hour or so."

"Oh!" her mother said, surprised. "Well, where are you now?"

"Still at school," Cady said, feeling a little guilty. She had been getting home later and later these days.

"I think it's a terrific idea, honey," Mrs. Winton said. "But try to get back by dinner, okay?"

"Okay," Cady said. She hesitated, then she turned slightly so that her back was to Laura. "Could you call Nana's house and say I'll be over late, today?"

"I was just over there, darling. She's sound asleep," her mother said gently.

"Well, call anyway, okay?" Cady said, her voice rising a little. "Tell the nurse, or Mrs. Weber. In case Nana wakes up and wonders where I am."

"All right, Cady, I'll call," Mrs. Winton reassured her. "Now, you two go and have a good time."

"We will," Cady said faintly.

"Let's jam!" Laura said, the second Cady had hung up the receiver.

They scampered back to the truck. Laura's father was listening to the radio, a huge smile on his face. "Listen to this," he said to them, turning up the volume. He started singing along with the music.

Laura nudged Cady in the ribs as they put on their seat belts. "My dad is multitalented," she whispered, giggling. She made a face.

"Listen, listen!" her dad said, leaning forward. He turned up the volume and started singing again.

"You sound great, Daddy," Laura said.

But then she sneaked a look at Cady, and it was all over—except for the helpless laughter.

"I'm really wounded," Mr. McAllister said, sitting back with a pretend gasp and grabbing at his chest. But then he grinned, recovering instantly.

He started the truck—which felt almost as though it were full of helium, Cady thought. In fact, a giddy feeling was spreading throughout her body.

Mr. McAllister started humming along with another song, and the girls couldn't help it; they started shaking with silent laughter again. "Oof," Cady said, holding her aching sides.

"I know, I know!" Laura agreed.

• • •

After the short drive to Old Town, they parked the car. Then Laura's father took out his wallet and handed Laura some money. "This should be enough for you guys to have some fun," he said. He looked at his watch. "Okay," he said, turning serious, "let's meet at the bagel store at—oh, say at five-thirty, okay?"

Cady and Laura both looked at their watches, like spies about to start a secret mission. It was a little after four o'clock. "Okay," Laura said, nodding her head once. Cady nodded, too.

"Wish me luck, then!" Mr. Carpenter said, and he sprinted off down the sidewalk.

"Bingo," Laura said, grinning, and she held up two ten-dollar bills.

"Wow," Cady said, impressed. She couldn't imagine her own father handing out money that way.

Laura gave her one of the bills, and they looked at each other gleefully.

Alone in Old Town with her new friend, Cady thought—and they had money!

They tied their navy-blue sweaters around their waists in an attempt to hide their school uniforms. Then they strolled down one side of the street, looking in store windows. "Want to go try on clothes?" Laura asked, eyeing a slinky metallic dress.

"Yeah, right," Cady said, laughing. "Like you could wear that to open house at Arroyo."

Laura tilted her head as if considering this, and held out one sneaker-shod foot. "What do you think?" she asked. "Would it go?"

"I think we'd better keep walking," Cady said.

They were both hungry, so they walked into an ice cream store and ordered fruit smoothies. The tall girl behind the counter, who somehow managed to look graceful and pretty even in her silly uniform, measured and poured things into a blender while the boy who was her coworker pretended not to watch.

"I'd like to work here some summer," Laura said, her voice hidden by the noisy whir. "It would be so great to make my own money and have some freedom."

"But you can't," Cady said, "not until you're at least sixteen, I think. Maybe you could get a babysitting job or something before that, though."

"Hey, I could babysit your little brother!" Laura said, excited. They each paid the girl behind the counter and put some coins into the tip jar.

"Right," Cady scoffed. "You haven't actually *met* Russell, don't forget."

"Kids love me," Laura assured her. "Anyway, how bad could he be?"

Cady grinned and then took a big gulp of her strawberry smoothie. "You'll find out someday," she promised.

"We'd better hurry," Laura said, looking at her watch. "I want to go into the bookstore, and they don't allow drinks."

Cady nodded and tried not to slurp.

• • •

"What are you looking for?" she asked Laura as they entered the store.

"Something that costs less than seven dollars and fifty cents," Laura said, patting her pocket.

"Well, you're in luck—here's a whole tableful of books for under five dollars," Cady said.

"Huh," Laura said, already lost in the display of books. Her thick braid swung across her shoulder as she bent over the table.

Cady turned away, suddenly remembering Nana's wispy curls—and the reason her best friend's hair was so short. "I'll be next to the window, looking at the magazines," she told Laura.

"Mmm-hmm," Laura said, opening one of the books.

Cady trudged over to the magazine section of the store; the afternoon seemed to have lost some of its brightness. But she found herself picking up first one magazine, then another. They even had magazines in French here, and in German!

Rounding a corner, she tripped over someone's backpack—and nearly fell face-down on the floor. "Yahhh!" she said, staggering to regain her balance.

A thin brown arm reached out to steady her. "Hey, I'm sorry," a boy said. He picked up the backpack and slung it over one of his shoulders with a single smooth movement. He was about fifteen years old, Cady thought. He had a skating magazine in his hand.

"I'm okay," Cady said, willing herself not to blush. Cut it out, she told herself sternly.

The boy stepped back to look at her better. "You go to Arroyo, don't you?" he asked, grinning suddenly.

Cady smoothed her uniform skirt, hating it. "Yeah," she admitted.

"My sister used to go there," the boy said. "She graduated a couple of years ago."

"Oh," Cady said, picking a magazine blindly from the rack. Her heart was jumping around in her chest. So this is how you meet boys, she thought. Cute ones, too. Wow! "I probably wouldn't know her, then," she told him.

"No," the boy agreed. He looked at the magazine Cady was holding. "You like cars?" he asked.

Cady looked down, startled. "Huh? Oh—oh, yeah, I really do. I really, really do," she said, but she stared at the magazine as if it had appeared there by magic. "Really," she added.

"I believe you," the boy said. He laughed, but he looked a little impressed. "Cool," he said.

Cady turned to the magazine rack and selected another car magazine, even gaudier than the first. She couldn't back out now!

"Hey, Cady," a voice behind her said. It was Laura!

"Oh, hi!" Cady said, whirling around. "Um, this is my friend Laura McAllister," she told the boy. "I'm Cady Winton," she added, mentally kicking herself for not telling him her name earlier. Not that he had asked.

And what was *his* name?

"Hi," Laura said, shy and surprised.

"Hi," the boy said. "I'm Tom. Hey, another girl from Arroyo! How many of you are there, anyway?" he added, joking. He peered around the end of the magazine rack as if there might be a whole line of seventh-grade girls, just waiting to meet him.

"There's only us," Cady told him.

"We've got to go," Laura whispered, looking at her watch like someone in a play.

"Oh, right!" Cady said, her voice bright. "Well, bye," she told the boy.

"Bye," he said. "Nice meeting you. Sorry about tripping you up."

"Well, thanks for saving me," Cady said, feeling foolish.

Laura nudged her, puzzled. "Aren't you going to put those back?" she asked, nodding at the magazines Cady was holding.

"Huh? No, I'm going to go pay for them!" she said, as if stating the obvious.

Laura gaped. "Huh?"

"Come on," Cady said, pulling on her friend's sleeve. "See ya," she added, trying to sound casual.

"Yeah, later," the boy said, turning back to the skating magazines.

"Cady," Laura said, under her breath, "who *was* that?"

"Just some guy," Cady said, giggling. "Wasn't he cute?"

"My God," Laura marveled. "You go wandering off, and then you meet a boy like that? Without even trying?"

Cady shrugged, trying to look modest.

"Well, ditch the magazines," Laura said, laughing. "We really have to go."

"No, that boy might see them," Cady said. "I'm going to buy them. I can always give them to Russell or something. It'll just take a sec, don't worry."

Laura shook her head, amazed. "Hot rod magazines, Cady. What next?"

"I'll keep you informed," Cady said with a giggle, and she stepped up to the cash register.

Chapter Ten

Apology

"WHERE *WERE* YOU?"

Maybe Nana's question came through clenched teeth; Cady had to lean forward in her bedside chair to hear it.

"Do you mean this afternoon?" Cady asked, stalling.

"Yes, this afternoon," Nana said, a look of disgust on her face. She gave the pain clicker an angry jab.

"My mom said you were asleep," Cady said, still not answering her friend's question.

"But where were you?" Nana asked again. "I needed you when I woke up. I felt terrible! And there was nobody to talk with."

"Wasn't Irene here?" Cady asked, staring down at her hand as it smoothed imaginary wrinkles from Nana's blanket. "Or your mom?"

"I called your house, and you weren't there," Nana said. "Russell answered the phone," she added.

"Oh, sorry," Cady said, trying to laugh.

"He said you went somewhere with a *friend,*" Nana said, relentless.

Cady patted her hand against the blanket, as if keeping time to a silent tune. "I told my mom to call and say I'd be late today," she finally said.

"Well, nobody told me!" Nana yelled. She picked up a box of tissues from her bedside table and threw it across the room. As far as she could, anyway—and Cady was surprised at her sudden strength.

"That's not my fault," Cady said, her heart racing. "She was supposed to call you."

"But where did you go?" Nana asked, returning to the original subject like a ferocious prosecutor.

"Old Town," Cady mumbled.

"On a Thursday?" Nana asked, outraged. "Your mother never let *us* hang out in Old Town on a school day!"

Cady shrugged a little and looked at the floor. "We didn't plan it that way," she said, "it just happened. Some-one's dad was picking her up, and—"

"*Someone?*" Nana pounced on the word. "Someone who?" she demanded.

"Laura McAllister," Cady said reluctantly. "She's new."

"Oh, great," Nana said, sagging back against her pillow. "I'm not even dead yet, and you've got a brand-new friend. And your mom and dad are just thrilled, I bet. Couldn't you at least have waited?"

"That's not fair," Cady whispered. Her lips felt numb, as though she'd been eating snow cones all day.

"What?" Nana asked, her eyes brightening with anger once more. "What did you say?"

"I said, *That's not fair,*" Cady repeated. She paused to clear her throat.

"What's not fair?" Nana shouted. "This is what's not fair, Cady," she said, slapping herself on the chest.

"I know that," Cady said. "I—"

"No, you *don't* know that," Nana interrupted. "I'm the

only one who knows that! And all I want is for my *best friend*"—she paused here, making sure that Cady had recognized sarcasm when she heard it—"for my best friend to be here when I need her. That's all."

"That's *all?*" Cady asked, jumping to her feet. "All I have to do is to be here every waking minute that I'm not in school, watching you die?"

"I just knew you hated being here!" Nana said. Her face shone with a terrible triumph.

Cady ran her hands back through her hair. "I do *not* hate being here, Nana. If I hated it that much, I wouldn't come, would I?"

"How should *I* know?" Nana shouted. "All I know is that you hate being with me!"

"Well, who's going to be with *me,* did you ever think about that?" Cady yelled back.

"What?"

"You heard me," Cady said, pacing now. "Where will you be if *I* ever get sick or really, really need someone to be there—someone who knew me since I was a baby? I know where you'll be. You'll be six feet under!"

Nana stared at her wide-eyed for one heart-stopping second, and then—then a faint, almost admiring, smile appeared on her face. "*Six feet under!* I can't believe you actually said that," she whispered, shaking her head in disbelief.

"Oh, God, me either," Cady said, sinking into her chair, all anger suddenly gone. "I must be losing my mind. I'm so sorry."

"No, no, you're right," Nana said, reaching for her hand. She laughed a little.

Tears sprang to Cady's eyes. "You are the only person in the world who would think that was funny," she stated, shaking her head. "I'll never have another friend as twisted as you, Nan."

"No, you won't," Nana said, looking pleased. She closed her eyes. "So, are you really, really mad at me for croaking on you?" she finally asked Cady, keeping her eyes shut.

"Yeah, kinda," Cady admitted.

"I thought so," Nana said.

"You *knew?*" Cady couldn't believe it.

Nana shrugged modestly. "Well, I was hoping," she said, her mouth turned up in a quirky smile.

"Hoping I'd be angry?" Cady asked, confused.

Nana thought for a moment, "Well, hoping I mattered that much," she finally said.

"You matter," Cady said, almost exhaling the words.

Nana looked at Cady. "Hey," she said, "I'm sorry."

"Oh, Nana, you don't—"

Nana held up one hand. "Let me finish," she said sternly. "I'm not sorry about taking up so much of your time, because I'd do the same for you, and you know it."

Cady nodded.

"And I'm not sorry about getting sick, because that wasn't my fault," Nana continued. "It just happened, that's all."

Cady looked down at her hands.

Nana took a deep, shaky breath before speaking again. "But I *am* sorry about bailing on you, Cady. Like you said, I'm not going to be there for you when a best friend should be. Like when you get married, or have a baby, or—or who knows what else? For the good things, and for the terrible things, too."

"Yeah," Cady said. Tears blurred her vision, brimming in her eyes.

"So, do you accept my apology?" Nana asked.

"Yeah, okay," Cady repeated, blinking once.

This time, the tears fell.

Chapter Eleven

Trapped

——————

IT WAS THE MIDDLE OF OCTOBER, and Nana's beading craze was ending. "I can't focus my eyes anymore," she told Cady. "This stupid thing," she added, throwing her partly finished bracelet onto the blanket.

Cady looked up from the tiny beads she was fashioning into a daisylike flower. "Maybe you just need to take a break," she said.

"I need a break, all right, but I'm not going to get it," Nana said bitterly. Cady could tell Nana was talking about more than beads. "I also need a shampoo," Nana continued. She shook her head violently, trying to fluff up the dull black curls that were smashed flat in back and sticking up on top. "Did you ever see that stuff Irene uses to wash my hair? You can't even rinse it out!"

Cady bit her lip and inspected her beadwork once more. Nana was sleeping more and more lately. When she was awake, though, and when she was with Cady, she tried to act like her usual funny self. She was making the effort, Cady knew.

With other people, Nana sometimes acted like a little angel, almost—extra sweet, easier to get along with by far than she ever had been before. It was like she was a character in a play, Cady thought. Maybe Nana was worried about how she would be remembered.

But other times she acted so grouchy!

She couldn't get comfortable.

The phone was too loud when it rang.

But it didn't ring often enough!

Even the water she drank had started tasting funny to Nana. But what did she expect Cady to do about it? Silent, Cady put her beads away.

"You don't have to stop beading just because I can't do it," Nana said peevishly.

"No, I'm tired of it, too," Cady said.

"I never said I was *tired* of beading," Nana began.

"I know. I—"

"Let me finish what I'm saying!" Nana said, frustrated.

"Okay, what?" Cady asked. This had better be good, she thought.

"I—I forgot. *Thanks,* Cady."

"Yoo-hoo," Mrs. Weber's voice called out from just outside Nana's door, "can I get you girls anything to drink?"

Nana squinted her eyes and seemed to shrink into her bed. She didn't answer her mother. "Uh, no thanks, Mrs. Weber," Cady called out. "What's the matter now?" she whispered to Nana.

"She's—driving—me—*crazy*," Nana said under her breath. "My mother is driving me crazy," she repeated, as though Cady might have misunderstood the first time.

"Why, what's she doing?" Cady asked.

"What do you mean, what's she doing?" Nana cried. "You've heard her!"

"Oh, yeah," Cady said. But she didn't really know what Nana was talking about. She stared out Nana's rain-streaked window. Last year, they would probably have gone to the movies on a gloomy Saturday, she thought. Now, Nana didn't even want to hear about any new movies.

Cady couldn't help wondering what Laura was doing.

"Oh, my mom can be great," Nana said, as if trying to be fair now. She shifted uncomfortably in her bed and reached for a glass of water. "She does everything for me," she said after taking a sip.

"Well, that's enough to drive you crazy right there," Cady said, only half joking.

She tried to imagine what it would be like always to have your mother hanging around, just when you were at an age when you wanted to be by yourself more and more.

"It's not her fault," Nana said, and she started to cry.

"Nana, I never said—I didn't mean to criticize your mom," Cady said, feeling helpless. What did Nana want from her?

"You're not, that's okay," Nana said. She sniffled, grabbed a tissue, and blew her nose. "It's just that—I don't know, all I ever feel like doing anymore is yelling at her. I feel so guilty all the time," she added.

"Guilty? How come?" Cady asked.

"I don't know. Because I got worse, because I'm letting her down," Nana said. "Because I'm not ever going to grow up. I'll be leaving her alone, just like I'm leaving you."

Cady stared at a spot on the wall somewhere above Nana's head.

"And then some of the time I just *hate* my mom—for making me feel this way," Nana continued, "like this bad thing is happening to her and not me. And that's all wrong—this is *my* story. It's not fair," Nana added, frowning now.

"Yeah," Cady said faintly, but her friend didn't seem to hear her.

"If I weren't sick, me and my mom would probably be fighting a lot, sure," Nana said, "but then maybe we'd get to be friends when I got older. That happens, I've read about it in magazines. But now, *this* is all she'll remember," she said, waving her hand in the air. "It's like we're trapped," she added.

Trapped. Cady thought about the word. Nana was trapped in her body, trapped in her room.

Mrs. Weber was trapped here in the house with Nana, because this was happening to Mrs. Weber, too, no matter what Nana said.

And Mr. and Mrs. Weber acted like they were trapped with each other.

Maybe I'm trapped, too, Cady thought suddenly. After all, here I am, when there are a hundred other things I could be doing....

"I don't think your mom feels like you're letting her down, Nana," Cady said.

"Oh, maybe not," Nana said, restless. "Anyway," she added, "it's not like there's anything I can do about anything. *Period.*"

• • •

"Have you seen that monstrosity lately?" Mrs. Winton fumed at dinner that night. She tapped her serving spoon sharply against the side of the casserole dish and frowned.

"What monstrosity?" her husband asked.

"You know, the house being built at the top of the hill," Mrs. Winton said. "It's part Spanish hacienda, part English castle, and all ugly."

"Oh, *that* monstrosity," Mr. Winton said.

"What is this?" Russell asked, poking at his steaming dinner.

"Tuna casserole," his mother answered.

"Do I like it?"

"You love it," his father informed him. "Now eat up."

"Well, I think there ought to be a committee or something," Cady said, "to keep people from wrecking a perfectly good vacant lot with their rotten designs."

"But this is America, Cady," her father objected mildly, "with freedom for all. Maybe that's his dream house."

"No, I heard he's not even going to live there," Mrs. Winton said. "He's going to try to sell it right away."

"Good," Russell said, slurping up a noodle that was hanging out of his mouth. "Maybe somebody *nice* will move in. With a dog."

"Well, good luck in finding a buyer," Mrs. Winton said. "It will have to be someone with very peculiar taste," she added, and she chomped ferociously on a carrot stick as if to emphasize her point.

• • •

The days went on much as usual, although Cady often felt as though she were living two completely different lives. There was her life at Arroyo, where each day was packed so full with classes she scarcely had time to think. After the first few weeks of school, however, Cady realized that her classmates were mentioning Nana less and less. They were forgetting her already.

It was as though people could only be worried for so long before going on to something else.

But that was okay, Cady thought, as long as everyone left her alone. The time that she was spending now at Nana's house was her entire life now, she realized—her *real* life, that is.

• • •

From time to time, following their afternoon in Old Town, Laura McAllister tried to get Cady to join her in another after-school spree. But Cady had learned her lesson. She thought always now of how poor Nana would feel when she found out where she had been.

Oh, we'll never have another screaming fight, Cady realized, almost sadly—Nana was too weak for that now. But she could still be hurt, and Cady wasn't going to be the one to cause the pain.

She knew now why she was still visiting Nana every day, even though both of them had changed. It was out of loyalty, pity, and love. Nana had watched over her for years; now it was her turn to take care of Nana.

And it wasn't even that hard saying no to Laura, Cady told herself; with each day, Nana's room came into sharper focus, while the rest of the world blurred and faded away.

Even Laura didn't seem real, once the final school bell had rung.

Still, Cady's new friend persisted. "Listen," she said one day at lunch, "um, my mom was asking me if maybe you wanted to come over this weekend. It's Halloween," she added hurriedly, as if trying to explain as much as possible before Cady could say no again.

Cady took a deep breath before speaking. "No, I—"

"Wait," Laura said. "Listen to the whole invitation, at least. My mom was hoping we could take my little neighbor out trick-or-treating. Her mom has the flu. Hey, your brother could come, too! And then maybe you could spend the night," she finished in a rush. She tossed her head, flipping her braid over her shoulder, and took a big bite of her chicken sandwich. She chewed busily, as though it was taking all her concentration.

Cady looked down at her own sandwich, appetite gone. "Oh, I don't know," she began, "I—"

"Well, don't say no without even *thinking* about it!" Laura said, suddenly angry. "Come on, Cady," she continued stubbornly. "What's the deal? We have so much fun together, but whenever I ask you now if you want to do something after school, you say you can't. You're going to give me some kind of complex," she added, attempting a grin.

"No, it's not you," Cady tried to reassure Laura. "This has nothing to do with you."

"Well, what is it, then? Is it Nana?"

"I guess," Cady said softly.

"Look," Laura said, frustrated, "I'm not trying to take her place or anything. But I just moved here, remember. I don't know that many people—didn't you ever stop and think that I might be kind of lonely? That I might need a friend?"

"Nana's been my friend since we were babies," Cady said quickly.

"Hey, it's not a contest, is it?" Laura asked. "Okay, so you guys have been best friends forever, and I can't compete. I was stupid to keep on asking you over, and it won't ever happen again! Is that good enough? Now are you happy?" She stood up and brushed sandwich crumbs from the pleats of her skirt.

"No, I'm not happy," Cady said, her voice dull.

"Well, neither am I," Laura shot back. She slam-dunked her lunch sack into a trash can, whirled around, and walked away.

• • •

"I'll do the dishes if you want, sweetie," her mother said after dinner that night. "You go on up to Nana's."

"Thanks, Mom," Cady said, surprised. But she found herself lingering in the steamy kitchen.

"Of course, you don't *have* to go," Mrs. Winton said after a moment. "Do you have a lot of homework tonight?"

"Just the usual," Cady said. She reached for a dripping cooking pot and wiped it slowly with a blue plaid dish towel. "Mom, can I ask you something?"

"Sure, sweetie. What is it?"

"Well," Cady began, "it's just that you and Dad have stopped nagging at me, lately. You know, about spending time at Nana's, I mean. How come?"

"Cady, I hope we were never awful about it," her mother began.

"No, but you know what I mean," Cady persisted. She wasn't about to pretend they'd always been great about Nana's illness.

Mrs. Winton sighed and leaned back against the sink. "I do know what you mean," she finally admitted. "You're right, we weren't all that thrilled about you practically mov-ing in up there over the summer. But you have to under-stand something, Cady. . . . " Her voice trailed off.

"Understand what?" Cady prompted her.

Mrs. Winton turned and looked her in the eye. "How—how terrifying this is for us."

"For *you?*" Cady asked. "But Nana's the one who is sick!

I can see how her parents would be scared. Mr. Weber has practically turned into the Cheshire Cat. You know, it seems like he's gone most of the time, except for the spooky grin, but—"

"It's scary just watching it happen, Cady," her mother said quietly. "And I *have* been watching it happen. I've been going over there every day, too, just to help out wherever I could. Even though you weren't always aware of it."

"I was aware of it," Cady whispered. "Heather told me."

Mrs. Winton sighed. "Your daddy and I have known Nana's parents forever, and we've known Nana her whole life, since she was a little black-haired pixie racing around the yard. The thought of losing a child . . . "

"I know, but—"

"But it goes much deeper than that," Mrs. Winton continued, as though Cady hadn't spoken. "I was talking with your dad the other night, and I realized we've had this sort of superstitious dread, like *Just keep this thing away from my baby!* And that's not fair either to you or the Webers."

"But keep *what* away?" Cady asked, confused. "Keep Nana away? Nana's not a *thing,* Mom."

"No, sweetie, it has nothing to do with Nana personally. I'm talking about illness, death. We just couldn't bear the thought of you being exposed to all that so soon in your life. We wanted to protect you."

"But I don't have a choice," Cady said bleakly.

"I know, baby," her mother said, giving her a hug. "That's what we've come to realize, that you have to go through this, see it through to the end. We can't make it any easier for you, but we shouldn't be making it any harder."

Cady clung to her mother for a moment. Mrs. Winton had always been short, but Cady had been shorter. Now she had caught up; she was surprised at how small her mother seemed. "Mom," she whispered, "do you believe in miracles?"

"I sure do," her mother answered. "I believe it's a miracle each of us is born in the first place. Beyond that I think we should just be grateful for life itself, for as long as it lasts."

"But I wish—"

"Me too, baby. I wish so, too."

Chapter Twelve

Adventure!

———

"NANA, I HAVE THIS crazy idea," Cady whispered, setting her backpack down on the floor. It was Halloween afternoon. "Is Hospice Heather coming today?" She kept her voice low even though the two of them were alone in the room. A pot of orange chrysanthemums—wrapped in glossy black paper for the season—sat on the bedside table.

Nana turned her head slowly on the pillow until she was looking at Cady. "Mmm-hmm," she said, nodding her head *yes*. "She's here already, in the kitchen with Mom and Irene. Why?"

"There's just something I have to check with her," Cady said, smiling a little mysteriously. "I think she'll say yes, though," she added, poking at a drooping flower.

"Oh," Nana said, and she sighed. She had been quiet like this for five days now. The holiday—usually a big favorite of theirs—was not cheering her up. In fact, Nana wasn't even acting grouchy and unreasonable anymore, Cady thought.

Things were looking bad.

"Hey, remember when you told me you couldn't do anything about anything, period?" Cady asked Nana, leaning closer.

"I—sort of," Nana said, a frown wrinkling her brow slightly.

"Well, I've been feeling like that, too! And I'm tired of it. I thought of something you could do. *We* could do," Cady corrected herself. "To make things come out a little bit right. To sort of even things up," she added.

"Even things up, how?" Nana asked.

"Well, we could at least get even with that guy up the hill for building his crummy house on your vacant lot," Cady said, leaning forward with excitement.

"Yeah, and for making Russell cry," Nana added loyally.

She was sounding more like the old Nana now, Cady thought. "And for making Russell cry," she agreed, nodding.

"But how could we do that? What can we do?" Nana asked.

"You'll see," Cady promised. "It'll be hard, and it's kind of risky, but hey, we've got to do *something*. And anyway, Nana," she added, patting her backpack, "you need an adventure! We both do."

• • •

Heather and Irene helped get Nana dressed. They slid Nana's sweatpants up her legs while she was still in bed. Then Nana leaned forward. Heather detached the slender tube leading to the pain control box while Irene eased Nana's arms into a navy-blue sweater that buttoned up the front. Heather hooked the tube to the needle at the side of Nana's wrist once more and pressed the clicker for an extra dose.

Mrs. Weber stood at the foot of the bed, wringing her hands. "Are you sure we're doing the right thing?" she asked helplessly. Cady pitied her; in spite of herself, she was wondering the same thing.

"I *want* to do it," Nana said. Her voice sounded as though it were coming from far away. "Cady will take care of me, don't worry. And it's not going to kill me, Mom," she added, rolling her eyes.

The real Nana was definitely back again, Cady thought.

"Well," Mrs. Weber said, "can't we at least come with you on your walk? We'll stay out of your way."

"I think this is something they really want to do on their own," Heather said soothingly. "But it's not far, and I'll stick around until they get back, if it will make you feel any better."

"And I'll be here, too," Irene said. "We'll get her back into bed, and I guarantee she'll sleep well tonight."

Cady got the wheelchair from the corner of the room. Nana hadn't been in it for a long time now, so Cady had to move a tall stack of magazines and books that were on its seat.

She dusted it off.

She wheeled it over to the bed, and Irene showed her how to set its brake.

Heather and Irene pulled Nana to the side of the bed, helped her to sit up, then swiveled her body until her now-helpless legs dangled over the side of the bed. They held hands, making a basket seat for Nana, and—with one swift movement—transferred Nana from the bed to the chair.

Mrs. Weber went off to find Nana's sneakers while Heather moved the little pain control box to the wheelchair, fastening it securely with its Velcro straps. She handed Nana the pain clicker.

"I want some kind of costume," Nana announced, her voice shaky. "It *is* Halloween, don't forget. And Cady should wear a costume, too."

So she remembered what day it was after all, Cady thought! "What do you want to be?" she asked Nana.

"How about a skeleton? Or a ghost?" Nana suggested, slipping Cady a secret smile. Cady had to bite her lip to keep from laughing out loud.

Irene looked in the direction of the closet in which Nana's mother was rummaging to find the hidden mate to Nana's shoe. She lowered her voice and said, "Maybe you'd better think of something a little less, less—"

"Found it!" Mrs. Weber cried out in triumph. She emerged from the closet, her hair mussed, and held the shoe aloft.

"Hey, Mom," Nana said, "do you still have the funny hat you bought a couple of years ago? The one you wore to that party?" Cady had heard all about the hat, several times: made of shiny red straw, it was festooned with a broad black bow. Huge clumps of white silk flowers nestled around its brim.

Mr. Weber had said it made his tall wife look like a giant party favor.

"It's not a *funny hat*," Mrs. Weber said now, clearly offended. "I got it at Macy's, and it was very expensive."

"Nana didn't really mean it was funny," Cady fibbed. "Not funny ha-ha. She just meant it would be *fun*—you know, special."

"And hats are meant to be worn," Irene said as if quoting a well-known saying.

"Well, that's true," Mrs. Weber said, nodding her head. "I'll just go see if I can dig it up."

"Find something for Cady, too, don't forget," Nana called after her.

"I need to use the bathroom before we go," Cady announced.

"Better bring your backpack with you," Nana said, barely able to suppress a giggle.

"Oh, yeah, my backpack," said Cady, wearing her most innocent expression. "Thanks for reminding me."

• • •

Cady toiled up Pine Crest, pushing Nana's wheelchair. Nana held Cady's bulging backpack in her lap. It was almost dark. Cady stared at the back of Mrs. Weber's hat; its white flowers quivered slightly as the wheelchair rolled along the bumpy pavement. Her own long tasseled woolen cap was pulled down low over her ears.

Mrs. Morgan was in her front yard, lining the path to her door with sand-weighted luminarias, paper bags illuminated by small candles. She was wearing tight black leggings and an orange sweatshirt with Garfield—decked out in a Halloween mask—on the front. She looked up in astonishment as the two girls approached.

Cady could tell from the woman's expression how terrible she thought Nana looked.

"Hi, Mrs. Morgan," Nana called out. "Are you giving a party?"

"Just a teensy little get-together," Mrs. Morgan said, as if explaining why Nana and Cady hadn't been invited. "How pretty you girls look," she added, attempting gaiety.

Nana patted her mother's hat and nodded.

Cady swung a multicolored tassel over one shoulder as if primping for some goofy dance. "We can't stop," she explained as they passed their wide-eyed neighbor.

"We have an appointment," Nana said. "Have fun tonight," she added. "I know *we* plan to!"

• • •

They passed only one trick-or-treater, out early with his mother. The little boy came to a halt right in front of Nana's wheelchair. "What are you supposed to be?" he asked.

"I'm a hat in a wheelchair," Nana answered. "What are you?"

"A Mediterranean fruit fly," he answered promptly. "See my wings?" He turned slightly and jumped up and down, making them flap. His mother laughed a little nervously, looking away from Nana's wheelchair.

"Cool," Cady said.

"Well, good luck," Nana added.

"They're giving out Snickers bars in that house," the little boy said, pointing an already-grubby finger. "The *big* kind."

"Thanks for the tip," Nana said, and they resumed their climb.

• • •

They passed the Snickers house without turning in, however. "There's Yesterday, Today, and Tomorrow," Nana said as they paused by a shadowy bush. "Remember?" she asked. "From our last walk?"

"Oh, yeah," Cady said, looking at the plant.

"Purple flowers for yesterday," Nana said, "lavender

for today, and white for tomorrow. Only it's not flowering now," she added.

"No," Cady agreed sadly. "It's not."

Nana laughed a little and said, "I guess I get to have yesterday and today, but not tomorrow."

"No, I guess not," Cady said.

"*You* will, though," Nana said, her voice soft. "Cady," she added in a rush, "remember me, okay? Whenever you do something that's really, really fun?"

"It won't *be* any fun if you're not there," Cady said loyally. She was glad she couldn't see Nana's face.

"Oh, sure it will," Nana said. "Someday it will. And you'll have other friends, too, and do you know what? I don't even mind anymore! Just don't forget me, that's all."

"I'll remember you forever," Cady promised. "You remember me, too, Nan. Okay?"

• • •

Finally they were at the top of the hill, where the new house was going up. Nana was silent as they approached the site. It was almost dark now, and Cady looked at the house, trying to see it through Nana's eyes. Yellow keep-out tape was pegged around the lot's perimeter. Two NO TRESPASSING signs further warned people to stay away.

The empty house looked unwelcoming. A wrought-iron gate locked off what would one day be a small patio leading to the front door. Masking tape crisscrossed every blank window, forming huge Xs. The brick-bordered driveway was finished, however, and Cady pushed Nana's wheelchair up its gentle slope. She veered off the driveway and parked the chair behind a tall, tarp-covered stack of plywood. It made a good hiding place. "There," she said with satisfaction, putting on the brake.

"It's—it's a *horrible* house," Nana announced.

"Told you," Cady said with grim satisfaction.

"But what's it supposed to be?" Nana asked, clearly not expecting an answer. "Part of it looks modern, and the roof looks Spanish, and—see where the wall kind of tilts up at the corners? I guess that's supposed to look Chinese." She sighed.

"Maybe that guy wanted a little of everything," Cady suggested, "or maybe he's like the Morgans and all their cars—maybe he just can't make up his mind. Hey, maybe the Morgans will actually buy this place!"

"Oh, the guy who built it made up his mind all right," Nana said. "He decided to build the absolute ugliest house he could and then to sell it for as much money as possible, without even bothering to move in. And on top of that, he had the nerve to be mean to you and Russell, who were babies on this very street. He made Russell cry!"

"Well, at least the view is still here," Cady said. "He can't wreck that, anyway." They turned to watch the lights, which seemed to twinkle in the cold October air.

"You watch," Nana said. "He'll probably put up a wall and a big sign saying 'Scram—I *Paid* for This View!'"

"Probably," Cady agreed. "But at least there's not a full moon tonight."

"What—oh, right," Nana said, nodding her head in happy understanding. The silk flowers on Mrs. Weber's hat jiggled, seemingly in agreement. Slowly, Nana unzipped Cady's backpack, and with great ceremony she reached inside. She paused and said, "But remember, even though this was your idea, I get to be the director."

"Okay," Cady said, grinning. She straightened her knitted cap and put out her hand for a pale cylindrical object. "Now, where do you want me to start?"

• • •

Cady was afraid a car would come by—especially a dark green Jaguar—or that Heather, Irene, or Mrs. Weber would come looking for them if they stayed out too long, so she worked fast.

First she looped the toilet paper in swags along the patio wall, taking care to stay in the shadows. Cady could hear Nana laughing softly behind the stacked wood. "It's two-ply paper, nice and soft," she whispered as loud as she dared to Nana. "And it's scented! Smells like baby powder."

"I'm sure he'll appreciate it. Now the plants," Nana whispered back after she had caught her breath. "Get those poor bushes he tore up."

Cady saluted, then ran around and around the broken mustard plants, wrapping each one as though it were a mummy. "Oops," she said, coming to the end of her first roll, "I ran out." She held up the empty cardboard tube and made a tragic face.

"Don't worry, there's plenty more where that came from," Nana said, fishing out another roll of paper.

"Here," Cady said, handing her the tube. "Put it in the backpack. We wouldn't want to litter."

"Heavens no," Nana agreed. Cady headed back toward the house, fresh supplies in hand. "Try throwing it over the roof," Nana suggested.

"I don't know if—"

"Go on, try!" Nana urged.

The first time Cady tried, the roll went way up in the air—then plummeted back down and hit her on the head. Nana gasped with laughter as Cady rubbed her head comically, making the most of the moment. "Luckily, there are very few toilet paper injuries ever reported," Cady whispered solemnly, sounding like a reporter, and she bent over to pick up the roll.

At just that moment, a shaft of light glanced off a road-side hedge, signaling that a car was coming up the hill. "Stay down," Nana mouthed, motioning at Cady to remain crouched.

They held their breath.

A car appeared, slowing down as it passed the house. Cady saw people in the car point and stare. A person in the front passenger seat looked as though he was laughing. Then the car picked up speed and was gone.

"We better get out of here," Nana said, sounding a little scared. "They might call the police or something. They probably think we're vandals."

"So what?" Cady said, trying to sound nonchalant. "We're not leaving until I throw this roll over—that—stupid—house," she added, winding up as if for the pitch of a lifetime. "Look out, here comes—Nana's comet!" she cried as she let go of the toilet paper roll.

It sailed through the air as if in slow motion, unrolling perfectly as it soared, until a long tail was fluttering behind it. The paper settled gracefully onto the roof of the house.

"I can't believe you actually did it," Nana said, awed.

"*We* did it," Cady corrected her.

"Yeah," Nana agreed with a sigh. A triumphant smile spread across her weary face. "We did it—we pulled it off. But you thought of it."

Cady nodded, solemn. "It's not like I was about to let you down, Nan."

Chapter Thirteen

After

NANA DIED THE DAY after Thanksgiving. She had been in a coma for two weeks; Cady kept going over to see her every day after school, as usual.

Nana seemed to be getting smaller each day, Cady thought. Her skin looked almost golden at times.

Cady talked to Nana as though Nana could still hear her. She talked about Russell, about school.

She even told Nana a little about Laura.

She said goodbye one day; she knew it was time.

• • •

Mr. and Mrs. Weber were in Nana's room with Irene when Nana died. When Cady asked later, Irene told her that Nana's death was much the way Heather had said it would be: her breaths had sounded low, almost raspy for a while, then there had been longer pauses between those breaths. Still, one breath had slowly followed another until—just when it seemed most impossible for them to stop—they *had* stopped.

• • •

Irene called Cady's house an hour after Nana died. The Wintons had been sitting at the kitchen table eating leftover turkey sandwiches. "I'll take care of the dishes and everything, sweetheart," Cady's father told his wife, and Cady and her mother hurried up the hill to the Webers' house.

Cady's mother hugged Mrs. Weber, whose tall body shook with silent, tearless sobs. Mr. Weber stood nearby, watching her helplessly.

"Do you want to go to Nana's room, Cady? To say goodbye?" Irene asked gently.

"I already said it," Cady said. But she turned to walk down the hall to Nana's room.

"Want me to go with you, honey?" her mother asked.

"No, that's okay," Cady said.

• • •

Nana's hospital bed had been cranked flat. There was no needle at her wrist now, and all the medical equipment had been pushed to the corner of the room. The lights in the room were dim, and a candle flickered on a bookshelf. Nana's little brass bell sat next to it, tarnished now.

Cady stared first at the foot of Nana's bed, then let her eyes move slowly up, up the taut blanket, past the teddy bear clasped in Nana's hands, up to Nana's face. Then Cady was scared to look, but she made herself do it.

Nana's eyes were closed, but her mouth was slightly open. She didn't look as though she was about to speak, however. In fact, she didn't even look like Nana anymore. Oh, it was Nana all right, but in a way it wasn't. Not really.

"Nana, where are you?" Cady whispered.

She sure wasn't there.

• • •

Cady heard the Webers' front door open, and she heard the low murmur of voices float down the hall. One of the voices now sounded like Heather's. The soft *she—she—she* of the mingled voices soothed Cady, but she knew her time alone with Nana was about to end.

"Best friends forever," she promised Nana, and she leaned over to kiss her friend's hand.

• • •

Nana's funeral was held that Sunday afternoon. Mrs. Weber wanted Nana's Arroyo School classmates to be able to attend the service if they felt like it.

The little church was still decorated for Thanksgiving. Bound cornstalks leaned against the walls at intervals, and flowers—brilliant in their fall colors—covered Nana's casket. The Wintons arrived early and were taken to the third row; Russell had stayed home with a babysitter. Cady sat stiff in the hard pew, between her mother and her father, listening to the church fill up behind her. She vowed not to turn around, not for anything.

Mr. and Mrs. Weber sat together right in front of Cady.

The service was brief. The minister said something about Thanksgiving and spoke of how Nana's life had been full of celebration. Cady seemed to hear only every other word the minister was saying.

Once, she shook her head slightly, as if trying to improve her hearing; what on earth was that man talking about?

Nana's parents swayed slightly while he spoke, as if moved by a breeze no one else could feel.

• • •

After the funeral was over, Cady walked straight to the car and stood there patiently, waiting for her father to unlock the door. But he and Mrs. Winton were talking with other guests in the church courtyard.

Lots of kids and teachers from school had come to the funeral. Cady didn't feel like talking to anyone, though, so she stayed by the car.

But Laura McAllister and her father had come to the funeral, too, even though Laura had never known Nana. Laura walked up to where Cady was waiting. "Hi," she said shyly.

"Hi," Cady said, blinking in the sunlight. "You came," she added.

"Yeah, to be with you," Laura said simply. "Nana must have been so great," she added, looking around. "She had so many friends."

Cady tried to smile, but her eyes filled with tears.

Laura smoothed her braid over her dress, then looked up at Cady. "Are you okay?" she asked softly.

Cady thought about the question. "I don't know yet," she said at last. "Maybe. Probably. I don't know."

"Well, can I call you in a couple of days?" Laura asked. Cady's parents were approaching the car, heads lowered, their arms around each other's waists.

"Sure," Cady said. "I guess you can, if you want to."

"I want to," Laura said.

• • •

Mr. and Mrs. Weber went alone to the cemetery to bury their daughter. Cady didn't mind missing that part of the ceremony, though. After all, it wasn't the real Nana who was being buried; the real Nana had to be someplace else.

Cady was sure of that much, anyway.

• • •

The next morning, Cady woke up crying.

• • •

But the morning after that, when the phone rang, Cady had a story to tell. "You'll never guess what happened," she told Laura.

"What?"

"Well," Cady said, "I had a dream about Nana." She stretched the coils in the telephone cord as far as they would go.

"About the funeral?" Laura asked, her voice low.

"No, thank God," Cady said, actually laughing a little. "It was just a normal dream, with a normal Nana in it. We were talking together in her living room, and then—all of a sudden—she disappeared! Poof!"

"Nana *disappeared?*" Laura asked. Cady could almost see her fiddling with the end of her braid.

"Yes," Cady continued. "And I was just sitting there in my dream, on the sofa, and I was looking all around for her. She was just gone, though. But then, guess what happened?"

"What?" Laura asked.

"Well, I looked up, and I saw a tuft of curly black hair duck down behind this big old chair the Webers have—and I knew Nana was really only hiding from me. Just like when we were little."

"Ohhh." Laura seemed to exhale the word.

"And it was so cool," Cady continued, "because— you'll never guess—I woke up laughing!" Cady wiped tears away with the flat of her hand as she said this, but she was also smiling.

A little.